It's time for a knockout!

"Something wrong?" Bev asked.

"Oh, no worse than the usual," Jessica said sarcastically. "I was just thinking that my beauty routine will be a lot easier tomorrow night. After all, I won't have to brush my teeth anymore after they've been knocked out."

"Forget about it, Jessica." Sunshine stepped out of one of the showers and wrapped herself in a towel. "Believe me, you *don't* need to worry about your smile."

Somehow that doesn't sound so reassuring, Jessica thought.

"That's right. *Everything's* taken care of." Annette gave Sunshine and Bev a decisive nod, and Bev winked back.

What's going on? Jessica wondered. *One minute they seem like they're on my side, the next . . . watch out! Am I just being paranoid, or am I being smart?*

Jessica studied the faces of her friends as they prepared for bed. They all had one thing in common: Underneath their placid expressions, something menacing lurked in their eyes.

I'm not *being paranoid!* Jessica assured herself with a frown. *I'm not! They* definitely *have it in for somebody—the question is, do they have it in for Pruitt . . . or* me?

Bantam Books in the Sweet Valley University series.
Ask your bookseller for the books you have missed.

And don't miss these Sweet Valley
University Thriller Editions:

Visit the Official Sweet Valley Web Site on the Internet at:

http://www.sweetvalley.com

SWEET VALLEY UNIVERSITY®

Private Jessica

Written by
Laurie John

Created by
FRANCINE PASCAL

BANTAM BOOKS
NEW YORK · TORONTO · LONDON · SYDNEY · AUCKLAND

RL 8, age 14 and up

PRIVATE JESSICA

A Bantam Book / July 1998

Sweet Valley High® and Sweet Valley University®
are registered trademarks of Francine Pascal.
Conceived by Francine Pascal.
Produced by Daniel Weiss Associates, Inc.
33 West 17th Street
New York, NY 10011.

ISBN: 0-553-49224-1

Published simultaneously in the United States and Canada

Bantam Books are published by Bantam Books, a division of Bantam Doubleday Dell Publishing Group, Inc. Its trademark, consisting of the words "Bantam Books" and the portrayal of a rooster, is Registered in U.S. Patent and Trademark Office and in other countries. Marca Registrada. Bantam Books, 1540 Broadway, New York, New York 10036.

PRINTED IN THE UNITED STATES OF AMERICA

OPM   0 9 8 7 6 5 4 3 2 1

To Jeanette Heinrich Anastasi

Chapter One

"Promise me that if I die, you'll bring my ashes back to Sweet Valley and scatter them outside the WSVU building," Tom Watts croaked weakly, his deep voice reduced to a shadowy whisper. His strong, athletic body lay immobile. His hand, which had been loosely clasping Elizabeth's, fluttered to the floor as if the strength required to hold hers was too much to bear.

"You're not going to die, Tom," Elizabeth Wakefield said softly. She squeezed his other hand reassuringly.

"Don't ever forget how much I've loved you, Elizabeth," Tom muttered fretfully as she stroked his dark brown hair away from his burning forehead.

"Poor, poor Tom," Elizabeth murmured soothingly. Her sparkling aqua eyes clouded over as she surveyed the hideous red welts disfiguring her boyfriend's handsome face. She leaned forward to adjust the lush couch pillows that supported his head. As she did so her gold bangle bracelet, a recent gift from Tom, snagged in his hair.

"Ahhh!" Tom wailed. "Just let me die in peace."

He must feel awful, Elizabeth thought, her brow furrowing in concern. *But honestly, men are such big babies! You'd never see a woman carrying on like this over—*

"A simple allergic reaction," Tish Ellenbogen said as she bustled into the room, carrying a tray laden with steaming mugs of tea and assorted skin remedies. Her large silver-and-turquoise earrings jangled as she set the tray down on the flat head of a sculpted ancient fertility goddess, which served as an end table. She turned Tom's face toward hers gently and began applying a fragrant pink ointment to his irritated skin. "I blame myself entirely," she continued. "After all, I'm an aromatherapist. I should have found out Tom's medical history before I gave him my stress-relieving treatment."

"Oh no!" Elizabeth protested. "Don't be silly. It was an honest mistake. How could you have known that Tom would be allergic to essence of myrrh?" Elizabeth glanced over toward Tish's picture windows, where a jumble of planters filled with medicinal herbs and plants

2

flourished. Beyond the tangle of plants she could see the flowering trees of Riverside Park and the shimmering reflection of the setting sun on the Hudson River. "Tom and I would never think of blaming you—not after all you've done for us. If it wasn't for you, we wouldn't have been able to come to New York!"

Tish smiled. "Get some of this into you," she said in a motherly voice as she passed over a steaming mug of tea.

Elizabeth nodded gratefully and took a small sip of the spicy herbal brew as she looked around the spacious, elegant apartment that had been home to both her and Tom since their arrival in New York City. The classic simplicity of the floor-to-ceiling bookcases and Oriental rugs clashed cheerfully with the Mexican knickknacks and multicultural, spiritual artifacts that were sprinkled throughout the room. The mix was hardly traditional, but it was warm and cozy. *Just like Tish,* Elizabeth thought affectionately as she watched the woman tend to Tom. *She may be a little scatterbrained at times, but nobody could be kinder!*

"Honestly, Tish." Elizabeth put her mug down on the polished wooden floor and looked at her earnestly. "If you hadn't offered to let us stay here, I would never have had the chance to see my play produced off-Broadway."

Elizabeth had been thrilled to be one of three students selected for the prestigious Miller

Huttleby Theater Fellowship. The fellowship included round-trip, first-class airfare to New York, a daily stipend, and the chance to put on a full-scale production of her play, *Two Sides to Every Story,* which she had written as an assignment for her modern dramatic theory seminar at Sweet Valley University, where she and Tom were both students.

Too bad the Miller Huttleby people didn't think about covering the extras—like living arrangements! Elizabeth thought wryly. *I was sure I'd have to turn down the fellowship until Mom remembered Tish.* Tish Ellenbogen, one of Alice Wakefield's favorite sorority sisters, was divorced and living with her two daughters in a three-bedroom apartment on Manhattan's Upper West Side. When Mrs. Wakefield had contacted her, Tish had insisted on playing host to Elizabeth and Tom; she had plenty of room since her daughters were away for the summer.

"Oh, you kids are too sweet," Tish said as she finished applying the salve to Tom's hives. "I've certainly enjoyed having you here. I adore having company to care for." She screwed the cap on the ointment and pushed her salt-and-pepper-streaked hair back into its habitually messy bun. "And it's been a real treat for me to see you all grown up and in love, Elizabeth," she added with a warm smile at Tom.

It certainly seems that way, Elizabeth thought as

she squeezed Tom's hand. When Tom had decided to leave behind his internship at Action 5 News and come to New York with her, she was anxious about how Tish would cope with having both her *and* her boyfriend under the same roof. Was she ever in for a surprise!

Elizabeth blushed as she remembered her first night in Manhattan. Tish had been shocked—by the fact that Elizabeth and Tom *wouldn't* be sharing a room! During their first dinner together Tish had openly discussed the relative merits of virginity versus free love, and Tom had clearly been entertained by the sight of Elizabeth flushing bright red and pushing her food around in near humiliation.

Of course Tom was only too happy to have Tish on his side—he's more than ready to make love, Elizabeth recalled, flushing more deeply still as she remembered how close she had come to fulfilling Tom's dream. *I thought I was too—but I wasn't! Still, the summer isn't over yet. . . .* A bittersweet smile tugged at the corners of Elizabeth's mouth as she imagined what it would feel like to be crushed against Tom's bare chest with his hands—

"Something funny?" Tom asked, quirking an eyebrow and sounding more like his old self.

Elizabeth shook her head, her blond ponytail swinging back and forth. "You seem better," she pointed out, avoiding his question as she passed Tom a mug of tea.

Tom sat up slightly. "I guess I'll live," he admitted

wryly, accepting the flowered mug. He sniffed at it suspiciously.

"Don't worry, Tom." Tish took a healthy swallow from her own mug. "That's just simple peppermint. It will help your rash to heal."

Tom looked unconvinced, but he took a sip anyway. "So, how was *your* Wednesday, Liz? Wasn't today a dress rehearsal or something?"

Elizabeth nearly choked on her tea. *Dress rehearsal?* she asked herself. Un*dress rehearsal is more like it!* Her cheeks flamed as she remembered how the entire cast of a play by another fellowship winner, Claire Sterling, had paraded on stage stark naked. *I knew Claire was pretty avant-garde,* Elizabeth thought, recalling her surprise at how pretentious and snobbish she and the other Huttleby winner, Gerald van Houten, were. *I didn't realize* how *avant-garde until today!*

"Uh, it was, um . . . interesting," Elizabeth finally managed to splutter. *"Interesting,"* she mused. *Well, that's one way to describe seeing Vince Klee completely naked and totally nude!* Even though Elizabeth only had eyes for Tom, it hadn't escaped her notice that Vince Klee, the young movie star featured in Claire's play, was truly gorgeous. *He's just devastating,* she thought, biting her lip. *Vince is so dark and smoldering, he makes every other guy around seem like a little boy.*

Screech! Mental brakes! she told herself, blinking his image away. *You're only supposed to have thoughts like that about Tom! But then again, you've never seen Tom the same way you've seen Vince. . . .*

"Elizabeth, you're bright red!" Tish cried. "Are you all right? You don't have any plant allergies, do you?"

Elizabeth touched her warm, rosy cheeks. "Plant allergies? Oh no, Tish. I'm fine." *It's not essence of myrrh that's making me blush,* she added silently. *It's essence of Vince Klee!*

"Well, then, you must be tired," Tish said briskly. "No wonder. You spent a full day in the stimulating atmosphere of the theater . . ."

Stimulating—and how! Elizabeth thought wryly.

". . . and then you come home to find Tom looking like he's at death's door. You're just exhausted, poor thing! I'm getting you a cold compress, and then it's off to bed with you!" Tish stood up and beckoned Elizabeth to follow her into the kitchen.

"I think you're right, Tish. . . . I must be more tired than I thought," Elizabeth agreed, avoiding Tom's querying eyes.

I'd better go to sleep before Tom tries to pull the truth out of me, Elizabeth realized. *Poor guy. He gave up his summer internship so he could come with me, and the most exciting thing that's happened to him is that he's wound up looking like a poster child for the smallpox vaccine. The last thing he needs to hear right now is how I spent my afternoon watching*

7

one of the handsomest guys in America walk around stark naked!

Now what was that? Tom wondered as he watched Elizabeth head for the kitchen. *I know Elizabeth, and that was a* blush *flush. What's she got to be blushing about?* Tom winced as he envisioned Elizabeth, beautiful and confident, sitting in a director's chair while dozens of studly actors auditioned for her. *Well, even if that was just a tired flush,* he amended, pushing the image from his mind, *she could at least stay up with me until this Killer Tomato from Mars rash clears up.*

Tom knew that he was being childish, but he couldn't help himself. Lately it seemed as if everything was going against him. *I gave up a great internship in L.A. so I could follow Elizabeth to New York,* Tom recalled with a tinge of bitterness. He pushed himself off the couch and began pacing restlessly. In spite of the "cooling" peppermint tea, he still felt unpleasantly heated, and thick pink ointment was dripping down his neck and leaving sticky blobs on his blue polo shirt.

Elizabeth doesn't even seem to appreciate everything I've given up for her, Tom mused, his brow darkening as he paused in front of the picture windows and stared out at the twinkling lights of New Jersey on the other side of the Hudson River. *I was so sure that this trip would bring us even closer together. I thought that when Elizabeth realized I'd* given up everything to follow her to New York that we'd . . . we'd . . .

C'mon, pal, just say it—that you'd sleep together, an impatient voice in Tom's head urged. *You know you want to. You know you can't stop thinking about it.*

Tom closed his eyes briefly. An image of Elizabeth lying on top of him in a cab just days earlier flooded his mind. *That's enough!* he scolded himself. *I'm driving myself crazy!*

Oh, really? the voice replied. *Isn't* Elizabeth *the one driving you crazy?*

Tom knew he would never force Elizabeth to do anything that she wasn't ready for. And while he didn't want to use his job sacrifice as a tool for emotional blackmail, he couldn't keep himself from feeling disappointed that his relationship with Elizabeth hadn't moved to the next level.

It seemed inevitable. Tom sighed raggedly as he resumed pacing. *Tish sure made it clear that she wouldn't mind if we shared the same room, and Elizabeth seemed like she was ready. . . .* Tom scratched his chin thoughtfully and ran his hand through his hair, unaware that he was leaving a wide swath of pink streaks. *Doesn't she want it as much as I do? Doesn't she wonder what it would feel like to be that intimate?* Tom shivered slightly as he wondered himself how it would feel. *How close would we become once there were no barriers left between us? Once I've caressed every inch of her?*

Tom couldn't help smiling as he remembered the previous night. He'd knocked on Elizabeth's door at 2 A.M. to apologize for an earlier fight, and they'd both been so tired that they'd fallen asleep in each other's arms, the blankets tangled at their feet. Even though they hadn't had sex, sleeping in the same bed had been incredibly romantic.

"What had we even fought about?" Tom muttered. "Oh yeah . . . Elizabeth doesn't want to have sex with me yet, *that's* what."

Tom's grin disappeared as he remembered their argument. For two consecutive nights Elizabeth had agreed that she was ready to make love. But the first night their plans were thwarted after Tom accidentally split his lip open in a speeding cab; the second, Elizabeth had pulled away from him just when things began to heat up, insisting that she needed to work on her play. Last night, when Tom began hinting around at his interest to pick up where they'd left off, Elizabeth demurred yet again—and Tom had accused her of leading him on. After she angrily insisted that Tom had been putting too much pressure on her, he'd stormed out of the apartment.

He winced, remembering the grungy bar he'd ended up in, and his rash flared up as the raunchy, sexist comments of his newfound pool-playing "buddies" came floating back to him. *What a bunch of drunken idiots,* Tom thought as he rubbed his temples, which throbbed thanks to the many tequila shooters he'd downed in the hopes of drinking away the memory of Elizabeth's angry, tear-streaked face.

"What was I thinking?" Tom asked himself. "Trying to persuade someone to have sex before she's ready is the kind of thing those beer-swilling Neanderthals would do."

I turned into a different person, Tom thought with a groan. *It must have been that aromatherapy treatment Tish gave me—it really pushed me over the edge.* Tom paused to study his reflection in the window and grimaced. *Face it—aromatherapy and Tom Watts are a lethal combination.*

After turning away from the window, Tom flung himself on the couch, spattering droplets of pink goo everywhere. "What am I getting so worked up about? There's nothing the matter between me and Elizabeth," Tom reassured himself. "There's absolutely no reason for me to be insecure."

Tom sat up ramrod straight with a sense of resolve for about two minutes before he slumped back against the couch. *Maybe things are fine between me and Elizabeth, but that still doesn't mean I have a job!* He swallowed hard, remembering the humiliating job search he'd been on since arriving in New York. *The best offer I got in broadcast journalism was slinging hash in a network cafeteria!*

"How am I going to get a job now?" Tom complained. "Who's going to hire me when I look like this? The only job I could get would be as the 'before' model in an ad for leprosy medication."

Tom turned to the fertility goddess at his elbow. "What's wrong with me?" he asked the voluptuous statue. "I'm in the most exciting city in the world with the most fantastic woman in the world. So why do I feel like the biggest *loser* in the *universe?*"

Jessica Wakefield's luxurious golden hair was in a hopeless tangle, her normally sun-kissed skin was fast becoming sunburned, and every muscle in her body screamed—but *worst* of all, her pedicure was ruined.

And who knows when I'll be able to get another one? she thought disconsolately as she limped to her bunk.

"Sergeant Pruitt is one tough customer." Annette Polanco sighed as she jumped up on her top bunk, untied her combat boots, and threw them to the floor.

"You mean *torture master* Pruitt," Bev Vernon amended bitterly as she took to her bunk beneath Annette's and ran her hands quickly over her close-cropped, bleached blond hair. "She may be the leader of our pack, but she is *not* all that."

"Six hours of bathroom detail," Annette murmured. "I don't think I'm ever going to recover. We sure are four lucky gals, ain't we?"

"We ain't," Sunshine Harris grumped as she

hoisted herself up onto the bunk over Jessica's. She began to light a cigar she had hidden under her pillow but gave up. "Forget it. I'm too tired to puff."

With a groan Jessica flung herself back on her bed, too tired for the moment to change out of her Florida Specialized Security Academy–issue black uniform. "Scrubbing toilets is *not* what I had in mind when I joined the FSSA," she moaned.

Jessica had been sure that she was in for the time of her life when she'd enrolled in what she'd been led to believe was an elite, glamorous training facility for bodyguards to the rich and famous. She sighed, remembering how the brochure had featured a glossy photo of a stunning young woman in an awesome cat suit guarding Vince Klee, an even more stunning movie star. The accompanying text explained how FSSA graduates earned hand-in-glove jobs protecting the biggest names in the entertainment world.

That's a laugh, Jessica thought, smirking. *I bet the closest an FSSA graduate ever got to a rock star was gate-crashing a concert!* She rolled over on her stomach and stared at the dismal barracks room, which was painted in a color somewhere between mildew and vomit. *I was so sure that this was going to be a summer to brag to my Theta sisters about. What would they think if they knew I was in Swampland, U.S.A., with my head in a toilet?*

"Look, toilet scrubbing aside," Sunshine

began, "the one thing *none* of us had in mind was getting stuck with an evil drill sergeant like Pruitt."

Jessica sat up and began tugging off her combat boots. *Just as I thought,* she noted with a scowl. *Not only is the polish chipped, but my cuticles are totally ragged!*

"Pruitt sure has it in for us," Annette agreed. "You most of all, Jessica. I can't believe she challenged you to a boxing match on Saturday—and you accepted! Were you out of your mind?"

"Don't remind me," Jessica begged, her heart sinking. When Pruitt had caught Jessica and her friends taking out their aggressions on punching bags in the gym when they were supposed to have been running punishment laps around the track, Pruitt angrily singled out Jessica and threatened to take her out in the ring, one-on-one. Undaunted and impulsive, Jessica agreed—but once she'd discovered that Pruitt actually had once held a Golden Gloves title, she'd quickly wished she'd never opened her big mouth.

"*That's* probably why Pruitt banished us to bathroom detail," Sunshine complained. "Did you see the look on her face? She couldn't believe you had the nerve to take her on."

"Doubt it," Bev chimed in with a yawn. "She hates us, period. We'd have been polishing porcelain no matter *how* Jessica reacted." She leaned across the space between the bunks and patted

Jessica on the shoulder. "Don't sweat it, Jess. You know we've got your back."

"Thanks," Jessica whispered weakly. *You wouldn't want to take my place for a few rounds, would you?* she added silently.

"Lights-out!" a voice bellowed from the corridor, and the barracks was pitched into darkness.

Jessica peeled off her uniform, pulled on her nightshirt, and collapsed back on the bed, struggling to bury her head in the thin, musty pillow. *Mmm, I'm dreaming already. . . . I'm dreaming of . . . a herd of buffalo?* Jessica wondered, sitting upright. *Where is that stomping noise coming from?*

"This is your lucky night, princess," a voice hissed in her ear—a voice belonging to none other than Sergeant Vanessa T. Pruitt. "I'm giving you one last chance to back out."

Jessica rubbed her eyes, wishing she could erase the hideous, shadowy sight of Sergeant Pruitt's face confronting hers. Pruitt's pointy, rock-solid jaw and mean, beady little eyes were positively nightmare inducing. "Yeah, right," Jessica sneered, even though her heart was pounding anxiously. "You're just *praying* I'll back out. You know I'm going to totally pulverize you!" She tossed her hair with false bravado.

Who am I kidding? she asked herself. *She'll flatten me in two seconds!*

"You tell her, girl!" Bev cheered.

"Go, Jessica, go!" Sunshine urged.

"Quiet," Pruitt growled. "You wouldn't want your little girlfriend to require *stitches* on Saturday, would you?"

Jessica gulped. *They shouldn't cheer me on like that!* she thought miserably, shuddering as she imagined Pruitt's leaden fist connecting with her jaw. *Are they trying to get me killed? I can't back down right here in front of them now!*

"Well?" Pruitt demanded, thrusting her jaw out even farther. "I know you're just crazy enough to think you can take me on, but do you have the guts? Do you have the nerve? Or are you going to back out?"

"Are you crazy?" Jessica shrieked. She gulped again, painfully aware of her heart thudding against her ribs. "Not only am I *not* backing out, Pruitt, but I'm positively *counting* the days until I meet you in the ring!"

Pruitt stood stony faced, her hands on her hips, while the barracks erupted into whoops and cheers. "Well, I'm glad to know that you can count," she said when the noise had died down. "But just in case you can't, the fight's Saturday. That leaves barely three days for you to get your sorry sorority girl butt in shape!" Pruitt spun around on her heels and marched like a storm trooper out of the barracks.

Jessica lay down and hugged her pillow to her chest, shivering uncontrollably. *What have I gotten myself into now?* she wondered. Jessica had always prided herself on being in excellent condition, but there was no denying that she had virtually no boxing experience; Pruitt could dance rings around her for sure—and put a few black ones around her eyes at the same time.

There's only one thing to do, Jessica told herself fiercely. *I've got to stop the fight before it even starts—or Pruitt will totally kill me!* Jessica gasped as the horrible truth hit her full force. Her stomach clenched as she imagined how much it would hurt if Pruitt landed a single killer punch on her.

Forget the pain—that's nothing, she reminded herself. *Remember, she said* stitches—*and we're miles from any decent plastic surgeons!* Clutching her delicate nose protectively, Jessica dove under the covers, her night's beauty sleep ruined.

Chapter Two

"You certainly seem much better," Elizabeth told Tom over the excellent breakfast that Tish had prepared for them. She nodded in satisfaction as she watched Tom take a third helping of seven-grain waffles and douse them in organic maple syrup.

Sighing with relief, she stretched lazily in her chair. The Thursday morning sun streamed through the windows and made pretty patterns on the dining-room table, illuminating the dozens of colorful candles and incense burners that Tish kept artfully arranged on its surface.

"I *am* better," Tom agreed through a mouthful of the waffles. "These are delicious." He swallowed and took a sip of the steaming chicory that Tish had served in lieu of coffee. "I guess I just needed a good night's sleep. So what do you think? Do I look OK enough to go job hunting?"

Elizabeth studied Tom's handsome face. His skin condition had improved vastly, and he looked smart and professional in his navy blue suit, crisp white shirt, and burgundy striped tie. "You look wonderful," she assured him truthfully. *But do* I? she wondered, pulling her thin lavender cardigan tightly around her body.

"Are you cold?" Tom arched an eyebrow.

"Cold? Well, no . . . maybe just a little." Elizabeth knew that sounded lame, but what could she say? That after yesterday's run-through of Claire's play, she wanted to cover as much skin as possible to counterbalance all the naked flesh that would be parading around the Maxwell Theater?

Elizabeth glanced down at her full-length chinos. She'd paired them with an oxford shirt in pale blue, which she'd buttoned all the way up to the neck. The combination covered Elizabeth as completely as a mummy's wrappings.

"So what's going on with you today?" Tom asked. "While I'm out there hitting the pavement, what exciting and innovative contributions will you be making to American theater?" He munched on some home fries and looked at Elizabeth expectantly.

Elizabeth rolled her eyes and rifled through her notebook. "Well, today I'm going to be blocking my play," she replied, glancing down at the production schedule. *Thank goodness,* she thought.

Then hopefully I won't have to sit through The Naked Vortex *again!* Elizabeth giggled to herself. She had once thought Claire's unbelievably tedious play, *The Eternal Vortex*, should be renamed *The Endless Abyss*, but this new title seemed far more appropriate.

But Elizabeth's glee died as she remembered the horrible job in store for her—or, more accurately, the horrible *actress*. Hildy Muldman, the woman who had basically been handed the lead role in her play by Ted Kelly, the Miller Huttleby Foundation's producer, was a complete and total pill who, when she wasn't insisting that her role wasn't rich enough, was complaining that the character of Phoebe was uninteresting and unidentifiable.

Even though Phoebe is actually based on me, Hildy's slams don't bother me all that much, Elizabeth told herself truthfully. *No, what* really *burns me is that Hildy doesn't have any talent—and she never stops arguing long enough to hear a word of my direction.*

Elizabeth sighed in frustration. *At least Ken Deal is easy to work with,* she mused, thinking admiringly of the actor she had cast as Gavin—a character she had based on Tom. *If he keeps putting up with Hildy's prima donna act, we might be able to pull this thing off.*

"Anything the matter?" Tom asked softly. "You seem awfully serious all of a sudden."

Elizabeth shook her head. "Oh no, not really."

She didn't want to burden Tom with her complaints—not when he had such a hard day in front of him. "I was just thinking that the actor who plays Gavin isn't nearly as handsome as you are," she added, her eyes sparkling mischievously over the rim of her mug.

Tom smiled back at her, clearly pleased by the flattery. "Well, listen, I better get going. The early bird catches the worm and all that." He stood up and put his dishes in the sink before collecting his briefcase. "Wish me luck." Tom stooped to kiss Elizabeth and tweak her blond ponytail.

"Good luck, Tom. I'll see you later," Elizabeth called after him lovingly as he shut the door to the apartment.

Elizabeth began clearing away her own dishes, hoping to get to the Maxwell early to go over her notes. She grinned ruefully at her outfit as she pushed up the sleeves of her sweater and squirted some soap on the cheerful pottery plates. "Well, at least no one could accuse *me* of being an exhibitionist," she muttered.

What does it matter, though? she wondered. *Who's dressed, who's not—who cares? At least* I'm *not the one who's sartorially challenged!*

"Ugh! What is this? Stewed cardboard?" Jessica made a face at the tin bowl of brown goo the server plunked on her tray as she made her way through the mess hall line.

"Maybe it's not as bad as it looks," Annette suggested, sniffing suspiciously at her spoon.

"Well, I'm not going to even try," Sunshine said as they sat down at one of the battered tables.

"Actually it's even *worse* than it looks," Bev said, pushing her dish away and busying herself by playing air drums with her silverware.

Jessica paused in the act of pushing away her own dish. *What am I doing?* she wondered. *Maybe this stuff tastes like garbage, but I'm going to have to keep up my strength for Saturday night.* Jessica pulled the bowl back toward her and began spooning into the brown goo.

Like everything else at FSSA, the food was a major disappointment. Jessica could have sworn that there had been some mention in the brochure of a classically trained French chef who specialized in creating nutritious menus for star athletes and top stunt people. *Yeah, right,* Jessica thought with a sneer. *The last menu this "chef" created was probably in some state penitentiary!* She swallowed a mouthful of cardboard casserole and nearly gagged. "Ugh! I must be still asleep—only something out of a nightmare could taste this bad!"

"I would have thought that with each of us paying ten thousand dollars tuition, they could afford to serve us something better than dog food," Sunshine drawled.

"*That's* what this reminds me of!" Annette cried. "Puppy Chow!" She turned slightly green and hurriedly reached for a glass of water.

"How would *you* know?" Bev asked with a chuckle.

Maybe if I just eat this whole bowl and everyone else's too, I'll be too sick to fight, Jessica reasoned as she choked on another mouthful, her eyes closed to help lessen the taste. *But yuck, which is worse? Getting creamed by Pruitt or downing extra helpings of blow-chunks chowder?*

"You're not really going to eat that, are you?" Sunshine asked as she chewed on an unlit cigar and looked at Jessica incredulously.

Jessica tried to smile, but the nausea swirling in her stomach made it more of a grimace. "I need to keep my strength up for the boxing match," she managed to splutter.

Suddenly they were interrupted by the pounding of a gavel.

"That must be Commander Phipps," Bev exclaimed, gesturing toward the podium.

Jessica turned to look at Commander Phipps. He was an imposing figure in full dress uniform with FSSA embroidered in scarlet over the pocket. Pruitt scurried nearby, setting up a microphone and a glass of water within easy reach. Although Jessica had heard a lot about Commander Phipps, this was her first glimpse of him, and she wasn't sure exactly what his role was at the training camp.

There's something awfully mysterious about him, she mused. As she stared up at the podium Jessica had to admit that so far he was the only thing at FSSA that even came close to living up to the extravagant claims made in the brochure. *He certainly seems like more of a born leader than Pruitt is,* she realized, her mouth twisting in a smile as she watched the unusual spectacle of Pruitt getting flustered.

"Jeez," Annette muttered. "You'd think she could set up a microphone without dropping it ten times." She sneezed out, "Fumble fingers!" from behind her hand.

Jessica snickered as Pruitt, growing redder by the minute, picked up the microphone only to knock over the glass of water. Finally she managed to get everything under control, and Jessica leaned forward, intent on catching the commander's words.

"Many of you joined FSSA in the hopes of achieving a special degree of skill," Phipps intoned into the microphone. "A degree of skill that would enable you to work at the top levels of the security industry, as highly paid bodyguards to the stars or as elite undercover agents." He paused dramatically. The entire room was silent, hanging on his every word.

"Not all of you will be able to pursue that dream," he continued, oblivious to the sighs of disappointment that followed his pronouncement. "Few have the guts and determination, not to mention the physical prowess, required to make it.

For those special few I'm pleased to announce that recruiters from several top-notch security firms will be visiting next Monday to interview trainees. Only the top ten percent in each class will be allowed the privilege of early interviewing." Commander Phipps took a list out of his pocket and scanned it as an excited buzz broke out over the mess hall.

"Cooooool," Jessica murmured, glancing at her equally wide-eyed, openmouthed friends.

Bev bounced up and down in her seat. "Do you think that means—"

"Ssh!" Annette interrupted. "He's starting to read the names from C class!"

"That's us!" Sunshine whispered excitedly.

Jessica crossed her fingers for good luck as she strained to hear Commander Phipps over the anxious chatter.

"Haley, Harris . . ."

"That's me, baby!" Sunshine cheered, a broad grin on her face.

"Patterson, Polanco . . ."

"Me too!" Annette's eyes widened as she high-fived Sunshine.

Jessica swallowed hard. *Why does my name always have to come last?* she lamented. *I hate suspense!*

"Van Dyke, Vernon . . ."

"Yes!" Bev raised a victory fist in the air.

"Waggoner . . ."

C'mon, Jessica urged silently. *My name's just got to be on that list!*

"Wakefield . . ."

"Yahooo!" Jessica shrieked. *I knew it!* she cheered silently. *I'll be out of here quicker than it takes for a French manicure to dry!*

"I wouldn't get too excited too soon," Sunshine cautioned, eyeing the expression on Jessica's face.

"Why not?" Jessica demanded. "I can interview with the best of them!" She held her head high and imagined the impression she'd make on the recruiter. *I'll go with the windblown look,* she resolved, pulling on the single long braid she was forced to wear during training. *It'll show off my adventurous side.* She looked down at her FSSA-issue black jumpsuit admiringly. Although she would have preferred it to have been made out of silk instead of a rayon blend, there was no denying that the cut showed off her slim curves, and the color was a perfect contrast to the brightness of her blond hair. She nodded in satisfaction, but her expression dimmed as she mentally reviewed her makeup supplies.

I have a lot of blush left and some of that bronze lipstick, but that's more of a poolside-leopard-bikini shade. . . . I've got it! She snapped her fingers. *Ravishing Red—that's sexy and strong. Perfect for escorting Vince Klee to all those award ceremonies—*

"Oh, I have no doubt that you really shine in

one-on-one situations, Jess," Sunshine said dryly, interrupting her thoughts. "But Pruitt would do anything to sabotage you. My advice is to keep your head low until Monday."

"I hear you," Jessica insisted, still lost in her Vince Klee daydream. They were strolling up the red carpet—he looking more foxy than ever in an Arturo Fuqui tux, she in a lacy beaded number made especially for her by Lucinda Collinsworth— when suddenly a beady-eyed woman with premature crow's-feet came rushing out of the crowd wearing boxing gloves . . .

"Oh no!" Jessica gasped. "The boxing match— it's on Saturday!" She covered her face with her hands. *There's no way I can shine in an interview wearing a full-body cast*, she lamented. *Pruitt has* already *sabotaged me!*

If things keep going on like this, I won't just need a job, Tom thought as he wearily dragged his aching feet along the blazingly hot sidewalk. *I'll need a job that comes with an all-expenses-paid vacation to the Bahamas!* He'd been hitting the streets for hours, and the charm of job hunting had worn painfully thin.

"If there was a TV job available within a fifty-mile radius, I'd have found it by now," Tom moaned, wiping his brow. "At this point I'll take anything—anything *but* pounding the pavement a minute more."

And I thought southern California was hot, Tom thought with a bitter laugh as he tugged at the collar of his sweat-stained shirt. He'd taken his jacket off long ago, and now it hung limply over his arm. His tie was askew, and the burgundy print was stained with mustard from an earlier collision with a hot dog cart.

Maybe I should *have taken that job at* Poodles in Print, Tom mused. *Nah, writing copy for a dog magazine just doesn't cut it. Still, it is closer to journalism than that gig setting up type. Maybe if I—*

"Hey, watch it!" Tom yelled as a bike messenger zoomed dangerously toward him. His cry was drowned out by a nearby, earsplittingly loud boom box, and the biker sideswiped him anyway, sending Tom flying facedown on the sidewalk. His briefcase spilled open and his resumes tumbled out.

"Hey, c'mon, don't step on that!" Tom pleaded as he scrambled to grab his resumes from underneath the parade of passing feet, but it was a losing battle. The few resumes he managed to recover were hopelessly scuffed and marred with footprints.

"Ow!" Tom yelled as a cowboy boot came crunching down on his knuckles. He struggled to his feet just in time to avoid being hit with a wad of gum spit out by a friendly teenager on in-line skates. Tom leaned back against a wall and gasped

29

for breath as he clutched his mangled resumes to his chest.

A tinkling sound caught his attention. "What the . . . ," he began, looking down at his feet to see his open briefcase rapidly filling up with pennies and other loose change courtesy of well-meaning passersby.

A sweet-faced older woman stopped and smiled kindly at Tom. "Don't let the wicked city get you down," she advised, pressing a pamphlet into his hand. "You're too young to give up hope, son."

Tom glanced at the lurid cover of the pamphlet: Bright red gothic lettering urged fallen sinners to atone. Groaning, he crumpled it up in his fist and looked at his watch.

"It's only eleven in the morning," Tom moaned, "and it's already one of the top-ten worst days of my life." He scooped up his briefcase and jacket, his face flaming with embarrassment, and hurried around the corner.

He took a subway map out of the breast pocket of his jacket. *Maybe I've just been looking in the wrong areas,* he thought as he studied the map. *Midtown is way too frantic, and the Upper East Side is way too uptight.* He looked up at the nearest street sign and smiled. Thirty-fourth Street and Seventh Avenue! He was only a few blocks away from Chelsea—and from what he'd read in *The New York Times,* it sounded like a hip, up-and-coming neighborhood, certain to be home to alternative newspapers and left-wing intellectual journals that were too "inside" to advertise in the classifieds.

Squaring his shoulders, Tom headed down Seventh Avenue with newfound determination, his briefcase jingling all the way.

Chapter Three

"I'm sorry, but the energy in this room just doesn't feel *pure*," Hildy Muldman complained as she theatrically held one hand to her brow. The spotlight emphasized the prissiness in her expression. "My aura is being *contaminated*."

Too bad Hildy can't bring that much drama to her performance, Elizabeth thought ruefully as her lead actress posed on the stage in one of the Maxwell's rehearsal rooms. "I'm sorry, Hildy. I understand it's hard to concentrate with all the stuff going on around here."

Admittedly there *was* a lot of hustle and bustle. Techs scurried back and forth carrying pieces of various sets, and lighting technicians were dragging wires through the hall. But it certainly wasn't enough to disturb Hildy's aura—not to Elizabeth anyway. It was just a convenient excuse to use on Hildy, even though Elizabeth's will to appease her was growing weaker by the second.

Elizabeth clapped. "OK, Hildy—do you think you can take it back to where Phoebe says, 'If you scoop me, Gavin, it will be the last thing you do'?" She consulted the notebook on her lap with a flashlight pen. "I'd like you to move toward Ken on that line."

"I don't think you *understand*." Hildy tossed her head in irritation. She tried to cross her arms in front of her chest, but the strange cuff links she wore—Elizabeth suspected they were actually dog tags—got caught in her long, frizzy hair. "I'm feeling *blocked*," Hildy continued with a scowl as she tried to free her wrists from the tangle. "I need to take a five-minute break to *reconnect* with my *chi;* otherwise I won't be able to *merge* fully with the character."

Ken let out a snort and rolled his eyes. "Do you really think that's necessary, Elizabeth?" he asked. "It would be nice if we could get this scene blocked sometime this decade."

Hildy shot him a look but refrained from saying anything. She pranced by him, holding her head high.

Ken obviously doesn't think much of Hildy, Elizabeth realized miserably. *But it looks like he doesn't think much of my ability to direct either!* "Sorry, Ken," she apologized sincerely. "Why don't you grab a cup of coffee?"

Ken shrugged and left the stage.

Elizabeth looked down at the notebook in her lap again, trying to make some sense out of the diagram she'd drawn. *Let's see, I want Phoebe to be behind Gavin's desk on that line so she can steal the file....*

"*The Eternal Vortex* is killing me," a voice hissed in her ear.

"Huh?" Elizabeth drew back, startled to see the anxious face of Gerald van Houten hovering next to hers. His teeth were grinding so violently, she feared he might bite her ear. "Yeah, I know what you mean," she concurred. "It *is* quite . . . something." Elizabeth didn't want to be catty, but she couldn't keep the sarcastic tone out of her voice.

"I mean it's just *outrageous*," Gerald continued as he took a seat and smoothed back the ponytail he wore to compensate for his prematurely receding hairline.

"That's for sure," Elizabeth said, glad that she and Gerald finally agreed about *something*. From minute one, he had shown her nothing but contempt. But clearly he was coming around to appreciate both her and her opinions—which, when it came to Claire's play, were pretty strong.

At the first reading of *The Eternal Vortex* Elizabeth had been shocked by how pretentious and nonsensical it was. The plot was incredibly difficult to follow, and even after witnessing yesterday's blocking, Elizabeth still wasn't sure exactly what it was about. Parts of it seemed to relate the feminist struggle to Sun-tzu's *The Art of War,* but it was hard to tell; much of the dialogue was gibberish.

But even if the story line weren't so incomprehensible, the play would still be overstepping the bounds, Elizabeth thought, fiddling with her pencil as she remembered seeing the entire cast forced to perform in the nude the day before. "You're right, Gerald. It *is* distasteful. That kind of sensationalism is unnecessary—"

"Are you *crazy?*" Gerald stared at Elizabeth as if she had suddenly sprouted horns. "That kind of sensationalism is *exactly* the kind of thing that makes critics go wild! There's no way we'll get any attention with her around! What about that scene where the actress holds a yoga pose while the rest of the cast sings Gregorian chants and turns cartwheels? How did Claire even come *up* with something like that?" Gerald's tone and the gleam in his eyes were positively admiring. In fact, he looked as if he were near tears. With a gasp he suddenly threw his hands in the air and brought them down in a gesture of prayer. "I'll say it first—she's a *genius.*"

Elizabeth squirmed in her seat. "Well, I'd like to think that I don't need to resort to tricks to get attention—"

"*Tricks?* We're going to have to resort to a lot more than *tricks* to get noticed by the critics, especially with an opening act like Claire's! We need some incredibly strong gimmick. I was so sure that *Leviathan Inferno* made a striking statement, but now I feel like a . . . a *peasant*." Gerald leaned forward. "I really thought that the court jester in my play is a potent metaphor for the game of life. And when the old man eats the apple—what could be a more powerful reminder of the fallacy of original sin?" Gerald shook his head as if he was finally acknowledging his own crushing failure. "It's just not enough. Not anymore."

"I still think that a well-written play with entertaining characters should be enough," Elizabeth protested feebly.

"Please," Gerald scoffed. "That's so *provincial*. I forget sometimes that you're from southern California." He flashed a smug, superior smile. "Art isn't about nice characters and tidy plots—it's about pushing people over the edge. It's about getting into people's faces and offending them." He paused for a moment as if deep in thought. "Actually . . . I'm toying with an idea that I'd like to run by you. But you mustn't reveal a *breath* of it to Claire."

"Of course," Elizabeth said politely, suppressing a smile at the idea of her revealing Gerald's trade secrets to the enemy. *I bet if I so much as said hi to Claire, she'd slash me with one of her spiked wrist bracelets!* she thought as she put away her notes and focused fully on Gerald. However different their views were, Elizabeth was a professional and always willing to help out.

"I was thinking of having a scene where all the characters speak in belches. There's something so *vital* about the emergence of one's own pure essence."

"Well, I think that might be just a little, uh, over the top; maybe a little *too* offensive—," Elizabeth stuttered.

Gerald arched an eyebrow haughtily. "Oh, come now, Elizabeth, surely you don't buy into all those bourgeois notions of *propriety*. Even you must be aware that the insistence on things like *soap* and *water* and *deodorant* is just one of the many ways society tries to push the artist down." He sniffed contemptuously. "Don't you see that belching is an expression of the deepest self, and things like *mouthwash* are just a pathetic attempt to crush the human spirit? Still, the belching *might* be too hard on the actors' throats. Do you mind if I practice on you?"

Elizabeth blanched. "Uh, Gerald? Will you excuse me? I just remembered a phone call I have to make . . . a *very long* phone call," she insisted, gathering her belongings and making a quick getaway before Gerald could summon up his "pure essence."

Tom smiled for the first time in hours as he took in the graceful, pretty town houses that lined the streets of Chelsea. Shade from flowering trees provided welcome relief, and the mixture of students and professional hipsters assured him that his assessment of the neighborhood had been correct.

He stopped suddenly as a large Help Wanted sign on the side of a building caught his eye. The Chelsea Vindicator, it proclaimed in bright red letters. His heart gave a little leap as he studied the notice.

"Positions available," he read aloud, grinning. Although the building was decidedly less attractive than any of the others on the street and the penmanship on the sign was less than copperplate, Tom's spirits soared. *With a name like that, it must be some idealistic by-the-people-for-the-people publication,* he noted, *devoted to exposing all the wrongdoers of the world. I bet this is the kind of paper Benjamin Franklin would have been proud of!*

With a surge of enthusiasm Tom plunged through the doorway of the building. He was slightly taken aback by the sudden darkness after the sunshine of the street. The musty smell in the hallway made him cough, but he put his hand on the rickety banister undeterred and started climbing the stairs. "So maybe these guys don't put a lot into interior decorating," he murmured. "Who cares? True idealists don't care about stuff like that anyway."

Tom reached the top of the stairs and pushed

open the door. The entrance office was less than inspiring, and Tom's heart sank a little as he took in the receptionist.

"Um, excuse me—uh . . . ," Tom faltered. *Is that a guy or a girl?* he wondered as he studied the receptionist's chalk white Statue of Liberty hairstyle and cartoonish face. *Forget looking natural— that hair color doesn't even look fake! And who* knows *what's hiding under all that makeup?* He shuddered slightly and tried not to stare at the snake tattoo on the receptionist's forehead.

There are *other indicators of gender, you know,* Tom reminded himself, but he decided it would be best to soldier on without looking for them. "I was, uh, looking for a job, and you had a sign outside. . . ."

Suddenly the receptionist began to cackle. *Was it something I said?* Tom wondered, confused.

"Sorry, kid, you don't look cut out for the Vindicator," the receptionist grunted in a bottomless and decidedly masculine voice.

"I don't see why not," Tom began, offended and relieved at the same time. "I'm capable—"

"Hey, Krull, what's all the racket?"

Tom turned to see a beefy man in a none too clean skull-and-crossbones T-shirt waddling into the reception area.

"Guy wants the job," the receptionist replied, gesturing toward Tom.

"Oh yeah?" Skull and Crossbones removed a

toothpick from his mouth and looked at Tom, who nodded dumbly. "We can't pay you at first, but any piercings you want are on the house."

"Huh?" Tom looked back and forth between Skull and Crossbones and Krull, truly befuddled. As he did so, his eye caught the sign behind the reception desk. "Chelsea Vindicator Body Piercing and More," he read out loud. "Any part, anywhere. You got it, we pierce it!"

"Catchy, huh?" Skull and Crossbones said proudly. "Of course, since we can't pay you, we could also throw in a complimentary tattoo. My cousin—"

Tom fled out the door, the sounds of raucous laughter echoing in his ears.

One and two, c'mon, give it all you got! Jessica cheered herself as she struggled through a killer set of one-armed push-ups. Sweat matted her hair and poured down her face, but for once Jessica didn't care. Even though she was on one of her few unsupervised breaks and would have preferred to relax with a good magazine, she'd hightailed it to the gym to pump some iron. The strenuous physical work helped take her mind off her upcoming boxing match with Pruitt. *And that's just what I need right now,* Jessica thought. *Because if I don't stop thinking about the match, I'll go crazy!*

"Nineteen, twenty!" Jessica gasped, and fell facedown on the gray gym mat. She was thankful the gym was empty; she wanted to work out her frustrations in peace. Usually Jessica enjoyed the crowded atmosphere—one of the only diversions available at FSSA was eyeing the totally ripped male recruits as they bench-pressed. *But I wouldn't even pay attention if Vince Klee himself asked me to spot him!* Jessica thought as she massaged her burned-out triceps.

C'mon, get up and do biceps, Jessica urged herself on. *There'll be plenty of time to lie down and relax after Saturday night. After all, you'll probably be in traction for a month!*

Jessica struggled over to the weight rack and picked up a set of dumbbells. She stared at herself in the mirror, noticing the swell of her muscles as she hefted the weights; she'd changed out of her jumpsuit and into a tank top and shorts so she could check out her definition and tone, which had improved strikingly in only three and a half days. *It's just my luck,* she mused. *Much more of this, and the line of my shoulders in strapless dresses will be absolutely ruined!*

She grimaced and put down the weights. "Maybe I should do a few sets of crunches," she decided. "A strong stomach takes a punch better, and the FSSA jumpsuit *does* flatter a small waist. . . ."

The squeak of the gym doors distracted her, and Jessica was relieved to see that her visitor was not Sergeant Pruitt but Harlan Edwards. *Not that*

that's an improvement, she thought, glowering as Harlan swaggered over to her. *He seems to pop up everywhere—like a bad penny!* At first she'd had her eye on the buff babe, but she'd soon discovered that he was a mercenary freak who was probably immortalized in his high-school yearbook as Most Likely to Go on a Kill-Crazy Rampage. To make matters worse, the little interest she now showed in him only seemed to increase his in her.

"Hey, cutie, what's shaking?" Harlan gave Jessica an appreciative smile as his ice blue eyes raked over her and lingered a little too long on her bare legs. Still leering, he sidled up to the weight rack, where he made a show of selecting the heaviest dumbbells.

With a snort Jessica ignored him and picked up the weights.

"What are you lifting?" Harlan grunted, turning beet red as he fought to hold up the weights. "Eight pounds? C'mon, Jessica, you're going to have to do better than that if you expect to fight Pruitt and live."

"Excuse me?" Jessica stopped what she was doing and stared at Harlan in the mirror. "What did you say?"

"C'mon, you must know that your little match with Pruitt is the hottest topic of conversation around here," Harlan grunted. He dropped the weights to the floor with a clatter and ran a hand confidently through his black hair. "Everyone's

43

taking bets on who's going to win. I thought that you had a chance, but now that I see you with those Barbie doll weights . . ." Harlan trailed off and shook his head.

"Just *what* are people saying?" Jessica demanded. She turned to face Harlan, her hands on her hips.

Harlan shrugged. "Well, people are pretty interested about why you would want to dust it up with someone as sweet and kind as Sergeant Pruitt," he drawled. "Of course, *I* know the reason." He paused to take a swig from a water bottle.

Jessica quirked her eyebrows. *Oooh, I can't* wait *to hear what startling theory Brainiac has come up with!* she thought grimly.

"Yup," Harlan continued. "The real reason behind the battle of the boxing babes is old Harlan P. Edwards himself."

Jessica's jaw dropped in disbelief. "*Excuuuse* me?"

"That's right, honey. I know I'm irresistible, but even so, I have to admit I'm truly flattered that two such lovely ladies would take to the ring because of me."

Of all the low-down, conceited pigs I've ever met! she thought angrily. *I could practice some left uppercuts on him right now!*

"Of course, I could always smooth things out for you . . . get Pruitt off your back, if you know what I mean." He lowered his left eyelid in a none too subtle wink.

I can't believe I ever thought this guy was hot! she chastised herself, infuriated. *He has all the class and charm of a used car salesman! He could win the Nobel Prize for sleaze!*

"For your information, Harlan," Jessica began in a steely voice, "Pruitt and I are *not* fighting over you, and the last thing I need is *anyone's* help—least of all yours!"

"Suit yourself, Jessie." Harlan stood up and tossed a towel over his shoulder. "But I'd hate to see that pretty face of yours messed up." With one last look at her legs he sauntered out of the gym.

That does it! Jessica fumed. *I will* not *be patronized—especially by a world-class creep like that! I'm going to train, and I'm going to win. And after I make Pruitt eat dust, I'll blow this joint. I'll impress the recruiters so much, they'll be* begging *to hire me!*

Chapter Four

I need a job, any *job,* Tom thought as he trudged eastward, his ears still ringing with humiliating laughter. *Correction—any job that pays in cash, not in complimentary self-mutilation!* His heart plummeted even further as he felt lukewarm droplets splatter on his head. Looking up, he realized it wasn't the omnipresent drainage off high-rise air conditioners that had pelted him for once or even bird droppings—but real, authentic *rain.*

"Great—and I don't even have an umbrella," he mumbled. "If I'm really lucky, I'll get pneumonia and die. Then at least my employment worries will be over!"

Tom dashed for shelter in the doorway of a nearby store. He didn't want to indulge in self-pity, but he couldn't help feeling down as passing taxis splashed him with filthy water. He closed his eyes and recalled a day back in California when a sudden rainfall interrupted a picnic he and Elizabeth had been having on the beach. Laughing and holding hands, they'd run to Elizabeth's Jeep only to find that it wouldn't start. But that hadn't bothered them at all. They spent the next hour and a half waiting for the storm to pass, kissing each other senseless as the rain made cozy pattering sounds on the windshield.

Tom remembered how beautiful Elizabeth had looked then. He pictured her laughing, sea-colored eyes and her golden hair shimmering with raindrops. Then the picture changed. Her beachwear became an elegant gown, and she was sweeping up onstage at the Tony Awards to accept her prize for best director while Tom stood nearby holding out a tin cup.

C'mon, things aren't quite that bad—yet. Tom shook his head and opened his eyes to clear the daydream, but the bleak sky and colorless, rain-soaked street didn't help him shake his grim mood.

Why is it that when Elizabeth and I were wandering around the city, it looked so glamorous? Tom wondered, recalling the magic of the Empire State Building and the hip energy of the East Village. *Now it just seems filthy and depressing.* Tom looked around in hopes of spotting a coffee shop to hole up in until the rain stopped.

Let's see, organic food market—no—religious bookstore—nuh-uh—adult movies—

"Gee, New York sure has some diverse neighborhoods," Tom noted wryly.

Comic book store with a Help Wanted sign—hey, wait a minute!

Tom blinked and looked twice to make sure that he wasn't imagining things. Sure enough, the sign was still there. "That's it! I'm going to get a job!" he announced with newfound energy. "Once I have some cash in my pocket and know the ins and outs of New York a little more, I'll look for a *real* job. But this should fit the bill for now."

Holding his briefcase over his head, Tom crossed the street. As he got closer he realized the sign specified prior experience was necessary. *Oh, c'mon, how hard can it be?* he wondered. *I know the difference between Batman and Superman. So some kids will ask me which is the latest edition of* Archie—*big whoop!*

Tom entered the store, shaking droplets of water around him. The warm interior was like a sanctuary compared to the wet outdoors, and Tom was relieved to see how much nicer it looked than the Vindicator. In fact, the store looked much nicer than Tom would have expected. The floor-to-ceiling bookshelves were stuffed to overflowing, and the customers perusing the shelves— mostly guys in their late teens and twenties—studied the merchandise with a seriousness that was usually reserved for rare books.

When I was a kid, I got my comics at the local

candy store, Tom reminisced. *Times sure have changed!*

"Anything I can help you with?" one of the three guys behind the counter asked, looking up from his task of sorting through an enormous pile of comic books. With his unkempt clothes and pen protector, he looked more like a physicist than a clerk in a comic store. The other two—one with Coke-bottle glasses, the other with frizzy hair—were leafing through a large reference book titled *The Connoisseur's Guide to Comics.* All three of them wore badges proclaiming them to be proud members of the Comic Book Society of America.

Maybe there's a little more to this than I thought, Tom thought, fighting down a twinge of anxiety. "Yeah." He cleared his throat. "I'm here for the job."

"Do you have experience?" the third guy asked, peering at Tom suspiciously through a mass of frizzy hair.

"Sure," Tom croaked. "I love Superman and those guys. I even had a pair of Road Runner pajamas when I was a kid." He cracked a smile, but it was clear his joke fell flat.

"Superman? *Road Runner?*" the guy in glasses asked, obviously stupefied, as all three guys looked at one another incredulously.

"Well," Frizzy began, "we'll need to ask you a few questions first."

"Sure," Tom replied. "Fire away. I'm from

southern California, and I'm a junior in college—"

"What's your take on Slimehog?" Coke Bottle interrupted. "Do you think that his descent into the kingdom of the Wart People in issue one hundred ninety-two was too derivative of Mucous Man's journey to the Planet of the PusEaters in number one forty-four?"

"What about Apocalyptic Ninja?" Pen Protector asked. "This store is nationally known for the extensive stock we carry on that series. How strong is your knowledge of the Ninja's family tree? Did you know that it was revealed that his ancestors were related to Unnatural Man when they were still foraging for worms in the Criton galaxy?"

"Can you tell us," Frizzy began as if his question were of the utmost importance to the future of the world, "in twenty sentences or less, the differences in the descriptions of Virtuo's three favorite weapons as they appeared in issues seventy-three and one twenty-five?"

Tom stared agape, powerless to reply.

"Of course, those are just easy questions—we don't want to insult you," Frizzy continued. "Maybe you can tell us something we *don't* know, like how it was exactly that Unnatural Man first learned to morph."

"Yeah, that's a tough one!" Coke Bottle agreed, giving Frizzy a high five.

Pen Protector bobbed his head up and down. "Good call! Answer that, and you could probably nominate yourself as the next president of Unnatural Man's fan club."

Tom swallowed hard and tugged at his collar, flustered by the heat of their expectant stares. *There's no way I can bluff my way through this one*, he realized, almost wishing he were back chewing the fat with Krull. *Maybe I should just level with these guys. At this point I've got nothing to lose.*

"Uh . . . look, I guess I'm not cut out for this," Tom admitted. "I'm really looking for a journalism job—television journalism in particular. You wouldn't happen to know if there are any independent production studios around here, would you?" He paused, afraid to make his next admission. "As you can tell, I'm actually . . . pretty . . . *desperate*."

The three of them stared at him in dumbfounded silence before the expert on Apocalyptic Ninja broke into a grin. "Yeah, I thought so!" he said, wagging his finger in Tom's direction. "You *do* kind of remind me of Jimmy Olsen. Sure, there's a studio not that far from here."

Tom's spirits soared. "Where?" he asked eagerly.

"Just down the block; you can't miss the sign. New York Network—that's where they do all that public access stuff."

"Hey, thanks, guys!" Tom said, grinning wildly as he headed for the door. *Finally I'm on my way!*

he thought, elated. *I'll get a hot journalism job, and then I'll take this town by storm!*

Elizabeth cowered behind her notebook in agony. She couldn't bear to even *look* at the stage, where Hildy was flying about like a witch on a broomstick.

At least the set looks good, Elizabeth consoled herself, peeking up over the top of her notebook. The stagehands had finally finished setting up, and Elizabeth had to admit that the results were terrific. The back wall was plastered with oversize headlines taken from some of the most important stories of the century. Reference books and literary journals covered every available surface, and pictures of world leaders were pinned up haphazardly around the room.

It really looks like a reporter's lair, Elizabeth thought, admiring an antique rolltop desk covered with journalism awards. *It's just too bad that Hildy doesn't know how to act like a reporter!*

Sighing, Elizabeth reluctantly tore her gaze away from a photo of Woodward and Bernstein and turned her attention to Hildy, who was prancing and posing—on one leg. Although Hildy had invested her character with plenty of bizarre physical gestures, such as constant twitching and hysterical shrieking, she'd never had a problem walking before, so Elizabeth was truly surprised when it appeared that Phoebe now sported a limp.

"Excuse me, Hildy?" Elizabeth interrupted the scene onstage, a crucially important part of the exposition. Gavin was seated at his desk while Phoebe showed him important information she'd uncovered regarding a congressman's wife. At least that was what was *supposed* to be happening onstage. But Hildy had chosen to do the scene another way. She dragged her leg behind her, her face set in a grimace of pain as she shook her fists at Gavin.

"Hildy?" Elizabeth continued, although the actress showed no signs of having heard her. "What's going on? You should be next to Gavin, showing him the evidence you've uncovered. Has something happened to your leg?" Elizabeth fought hard to keep the sarcasm out of her voice.

"I'm just trying to give the play some *energy*," Hildy snapped. "It needs to be *edgier*. I feel that it would really add some *depth* if Phoebe had a limp. Otherwise it's so dreadfully linear."

"I see," Elizabeth said slowly. "Could you explain that a little more fully, please? I'm afraid I don't quite follow you."

"Phoebe's allowed herself to be dominated by the patriarchy," Hildy explained as if she were talking to a two-year-old. "She's emotionally *crippled* because of it. Meanwhile Gavin is seated at his desk, surrounded by the psychological crutches he needs to hold himself up." Hildy gestured toward where Ken was sitting, his head in his hands.

"So, when Phoebe sees Gavin sitting there with that smug expression on his face, she realizes the sacrifices she's made for him," she continued, her voice rising in pitch. "The weight of that realization crushes her. Hence the limp. Of course to do the metaphor *true* justice, Phoebe should really be in a cast."

"Hold that thought," Elizabeth said hastily as she was momentarily diverted by a flurry of movement near one of the entrances. She sighed with relief as Vince Klee stepped into the rehearsal room, his powerful frame making up for the fact that he was actually shorter in person than he was on-screen.

He's so charismatic, Elizabeth noted, admiring Vince's dark, brooding good looks. *There's more drama in the way Vince walks into a room than there is in Hildy's entire performance!*

Before she'd even realized that Vince, the humble young actor she'd met outside the Maxwell on her first day, was actually Vince *Klee,* the hotter-than-hot movie star whose posters practically wallpapered the area next to Jessica's bed, Elizabeth had learned that he was not only talented in his own right but also incredibly sweet and kind and not at all swollen-headed. Vince was devoted to his craft, knew a lot about theater history, and even helped encourage Elizabeth to stick up for herself after a particularly nasty comment from Gerald had made her think of quitting. Most surprisingly, Vince seemed almost unwilling to believe he was truly talented—a fact completely at odds with the casual, assured way he carried himself.

"How's it going?" he whispered sympathetically as he took a seat beside Elizabeth. She rolled her eyes in response.

"If you two are *quite* finished flirting, we can get back to work," Hildy called out in an exasperated tone.

Elizabeth was glad that the rehearsal room was too dark for Vince to notice she was blushing. *I was hardly flirting!* she thought, embarrassed.

"Of course, if you want to pick up any *ideas* from *Vince,* be my guest," Hildy sneered. "Vince might just have some thoughts about *my* performance. He's certainly clueless when it comes to his own!"

Elizabeth shifted uncomfortably in her seat. *Why does Hildy have to be so rude?* she thought. *I guess it's because Vince is everything she isn't: good-looking, talented, successful, famous. . . .*

"Oh, I keep *forgetting!*" Hildy said, venom dripping from her every word. "Vince doesn't have to worry about *his* performance. Critics are always so impressed when Hollywood actors go *slumming.* I'm just a *classically* trained stage actress with a couple of indie features under my belt, so you see, I have to actually care about *my* performance."

Elizabeth cleared her throat. "In that case, Hildy, let's pick up where we left off. I'm not sure that I agree with you about Phoebe. I don't think that a limp adds anything." *Understatement of the year!* she added silently.

"Excuse me, Elizabeth, but I don't think you're aware of how dreadfully *boring* Phoebe is as a character. She's absolutely *unreal*. There's nothing *compelling* about her. Of course, if you don't *like* the limp, I could try something else." Hildy appeared lost in thought. "I could be struck blind suddenly!" she exclaimed. "Or perhaps Ken could contribute by wearing diapers and a bib. He could show how *infantile* Gavin really is."

Ken spluttered, but Hildy held up a hand to silence him. "*Really,* Elizabeth, the play desperately needs some texture, unless you want people falling *asleep* during the performance. Of course, that might start a new *trend* in theater. . . ." She trailed off, looking thoughtful as she wrapped a few split ends around her finger.

"I feel that Phoebe is a real character," Elizabeth said evenly. "In fact, to tell you the truth, she's partly based on me."

"*Oh!* Well, that *explains* it!" Hildy smiled sweetly. "Maybe you should retitle the play *Autobiography of a Semitalented Bore.*"

Elizabeth gasped and was about to read Hildy the riot act when she felt a hand grasp hers.

"Don't even bother," Vince said soothingly, his

dark eyes filled with concern. "You know how Hildy is. Even Steven Spielberg would have a hard time directing her. I think you're doing a great job—really."

Thank goodness for Vince, Elizabeth thought as she returned the pressure of his hand. *It's funny— just a second ago I wanted to curl up and die. But somehow things don't seem that bad anymore!*

If I never lift another weight again, it will be too soon! Jessica thought, closing the door of the gym and wearily making her way back to the barracks. *If that killer workout didn't get me ready to take on Pruitt, nothing will!*

For once the barracks looked good to Jessica. Although the walls were as drab as ever and the iron bedsteads still looked like something out of an orphanage, the atmosphere in the room was soothing. Sunshine lay on her bunk, blowing smoke rings up at the ceiling. Annette was working on a crossword puzzle, and Bev and several other of the recruits were playing cards.

I must really be wiped out if this place is starting to look good to me, Jessica thought ruefully. *Then again, anyplace with a bed would seem like Shangri-la right now.*

Jessica flung herself on her bunk. The lumpy mattress felt like goose feathers to her tired bones, and the itchy khaki blanket suddenly seemed as luxurious as the purple satin comforter she'd left behind in Sweet Valley. *Mmm, this is just what I needed!* Jessica thought. *I'll just take a little break—maybe four or five hours—then I'll take a hot shower. . . .*

"Attention!" Sergeant Pruitt's harsh voice rang out.

"What now?" Jessica groaned under her breath. She fell out of bed as everybody scrambled to their feet.

"Snap to it, Wakefield!" Sergeant Pruitt barked. She paraded up and down the rows of beds, a riding crop in her hands, inspecting everything with her eagle eyes. "Shoelaces undone, ten push-ups." She flicked the crop at one hapless recruit, who fell to the ground and began doing what she was told. "Belt buckle needs shining. KP duty." She continued striding back and forth, twitching her hips.

"And *you*." She wheeled around suddenly to face Jessica. "Bed unmade, posture contemptible, and personal hygiene questionable." She made a show of sniffing the air around Jessica. "In fact, you're altogether an embarrassment to this outfit." She fixed Jessica with a steely glare. "And your little friends aren't much better," she continued. "I don't think there is a punishment bad enough for you, Wakefield. You should probably be dismissed right now. But since I'm a softie, I'll give you a chance to make good. Report to the gym, now. Boxing workout. You and your friends. Hop to it!"

She's got to be kidding! Jessica thought, gasping in dismay. *I don't even have the strength to move!*

"Something wrong?" Pruitt quirked an eyebrow. "I could have you run a hundred laps around the track, princess. . . ."

"Boxing workout, *sir*." Jessica saluted, trying not to wince at the gleam of triumph in Pruitt's eyes.

They said it was just down the block, Tom recalled as he studied the address scrawled on a Wonder Woman postcard. He certainly hoped it wasn't much farther. Since leaving the comic book store he'd managed to loose the heel off one of his shoes, and he was having a hard time walking.

"It should be . . . this building." Tom double-checked the number he had written down to make sure he was right. After smoothing his damp hair and straightening his sodden tie, he debated ripping the heel off his other shoe just to make them even but decided against it.

Yet despite his haggard appearance Tom was actually feeling more confident than he had all day. After all, Tom *was* an ace reporter. He couldn't wait to be on familiar turf and dig his heels into some hot story. *New York must have more scandals per person than any other city,* Tom thought gleefully as he walked into the building. *There's got to be a hundred juicy secrets just waiting for old Tom Watts to come and uncover them.*

The building smelled strongly of kitty litter, but Tom didn't care. By now he realized that New York was full of places that would have been condemned by the board of health back in Sweet Valley.

I won't be too demanding about salary at first, he decided as he climbed the stairs, *as long as it's enough to take Elizabeth out to some really fancy restaurants. After I stun them with my first scoop, I'll renegotiate.*

Tom paused on the second landing. A door labeled Production Office in bright red swung slightly off its hinges. Plastering on his best interview smile, Tom confidently pushed the door open with his left hand.

The smile quickly faded from Tom's face, and he nearly bent over double with a fit of coughing. *Is there a fire in here?* Tom wondered as he waved his hand in front of his face to clear away the poisonous fumes.

Maybe I should give Poodles in Print *another shot,* Tom thought as he surveyed the wreckage of the room with dismay. The office was only slightly bigger than Tom's dorm room back in Sweet Valley and was crowded with a bunch of intern types. Unlike most interns, however, who hustled and bustled with excess energy, the group at New York Network seemed to be using the studio as a place to catch up on their sleep.

Tom couldn't help wondering if one of the

employees draped over a seat-sprung couch was dead. He was only slightly relieved when he rolled over and began to snore. Of the twelve employees present, Tom counted only five who appeared to be conscious.

He studied them a bit more closely, wondering who he should approach. *Boy, some of these guys make Krull look positively wholesome!* Tom noted, frowning as he took in the unwashed hair and grungy clothes of four men who were playing poker in a corner. He would have approached them, but he wasn't sure he could negotiate the masses of empty pizza cartons blocking his path.

Helplessly Tom searched the room for someone he could talk to. But the only other conscious person, a young woman who looked as if she was one of the Vindicator's best customers, was intent on waxing her legs. Tom didn't want to interrupt her.

OK, look, things really aren't as bad as they seem, Tom assured himself. *This place just lacks leadership, that's all. I'll get them straightened out in no time!* Tom looked around and noted that the editing table, although covered under five inches of dust, was the same kind he used in California.

Tom glanced at the wall, where four monitors were running simultaneously. None of the programs was transmitting clearly, but Tom was able to catch glimpses of them between the interference. The show on the first monitor appeared to address the usage of symbolism on *Beavis &Butt-head;* the second featured an earnest teenager leading a class in at-home tattooing. On the third monitor a drag queen was explaining how to make chicken potpie, while on the fourth, the worst-looking monitor of all, a bearded young man was talking a mile a minute about the direct influence of some guy named Jean-Pierre Melville on current cinema.

"You know, your monitors are really flipping out," Tom declared, unable to help himself. He gestured to the one on the far right, which was now completely white with snow. "Does your playback really *look* like that?"

"What do you care?" the girl waxing her legs asked belligerently.

"Well, I just thought you'd want to take care of it," Tom offered. "It's really not good for the equipment."

"Oh yeah?" One of the cardplayers looked up. A cigarette dangled from between his teeth, and he held another lit one in his hand.

"Yes, it's quite easy to fix," Tom said earnestly. "You just—"

"Hey, I know how to fix equipment too, OK?" The guy picked up a tape deck and began slamming it up and down on a pile of empty Chinese food cartons.

Tom looked on aghast as the intern continued banging the deck even after the screen had cleared up. "See, works great," he said with a grin.

Forget this! Tom thought angrily. *I could take the kitty litter smell. I could stand working in an environmental hazard. I can even look the other way if my "colleague" wants to wax her legs. But I will not work in a "newsroom" where the people don't even care about the news!*

Tom turned on his heel and headed down the stairs. *Look on the bright side,* he told himself once he was back down on the pavement and breathing smoke-free air. *I could always write an exposé on how hard it is to get a job in this town!*

Looking at his watch, Tom saw it was almost four, too late to continue job hunting. *Maybe I should meet Elizabeth at the theater,* Tom thought, smiling. *She'll cheer me up!* With a purposeful stride Tom headed for the subway, oblivious to the cars that splashed mud on him as he went.

Chapter
Five

"You know what this is about, don't you?" Sunshine whispered to Jessica as they trooped to the gym. Pruitt brought up the rear, flicking her crop double time.

"Of course," Jessica replied. "Pruitt makes the storm troopers in World War Two movies seem like kindergartners. *That's* what this is about."

"Nuh-uh," Annette joined in. Her pleasant face was creased with concern. "I think Pruitt's going to try and knock you out so you won't be able to compete."

"Either that or she'll just put on a show and destroy your confidence," Bev declared.

"Oh, *that's* all right," Jessica said stoutly as they entered the gym. "I don't have any confidence left to destroy!"

"Put on some gloves, princess." Pruitt sneered as she tossed Jessica a pair of boxing gloves. "You *do* know how to do that, don't you?"

I hate these things! Jessica thought with a grimace as she pulled on the slightly sweaty mitts. *They always feel icky, and* nothing's *more ruinous to my nails!*

Pruitt grinned viciously. "How about a little one-on-one?" she suggested, taking off her FSSA sergeant's shirt to reveal a black tank top and bulging muscles.

The last time I saw muscles like that was when I went to a Schwarzenegger movie! Jessica thought, gulping. *Who knew that no-figure Pruitt had arms bigger than my whole body!*

"Uh, no, thanks, *sir;* I think I'll warm up with a little shadowboxing first," Jessica stammered.

"Did you think I meant you?" Pruitt stared at Jessica incredulously, her hands on her hips. She twirled around and beckoned to a male private who was doing shoulder presses with a two-hundred-pound barbell. "You," she hollered. "Front and center!"

Is she kidding? Jessica gasped. *His jaw looks like it was carved from solid granite, and his arms look bigger than some of the giant redwoods back in California!*

The male private looked up in surprise but did as he was told. Jessica noted with delight that he lowered the barbell as easily as if it were a toothpick. *What a joke,* she thought with satisfaction. *She just picked that guy to scare me, but she won't*

66

feel so cocky after he makes her eat the flo—
    Wham!

Before Jessica could even blink, Pruitt had felled the recruit with one blow. He staggered slightly before tumbling to the mat.

"Is he still alive?" Bev squeaked, breaking the stunned silence as Pruitt nonchalantly blew on her knuckles. Meanwhile the recruit mumbled incomprehensibly.

"What did you say?" Sunshine leaned over his prostrate form.

"I said, what kind of dental services does this place have?" He groaned.

Jessica could practically feel the color draining from her face. Her head reeling, she stumbled backward into the storage shelves along the gymnasium wall, dislodging one. "Ouch!" she squealed as medicine balls, jump ropes, and ankle weights hailed down on her head with a loud, echoing clatter.

"That does it, princess!" Pruitt bellowed. "Hit the showers, and then get yourself over to my office—and start cleaning. You *must* be good for something, even if it is only as a *scrub*."

What a day, Elizabeth thought as she stood up for the first time in hours and stretched the kinks out of her back. *Who knew that directing a play would be this draining?*

Elizabeth gathered up her notebook and bag

and walked toward the exit. As she passed through the main theater she admired the red velvet plush seats and ornate gold curtains held back from the stage with satin swags. The Maxwell's atmosphere was so magical, even the disappointments of the past week couldn't dim its hold on her.

Just think of who must have walked on that stage! Elizabeth mused, looking past the footlights. *Laurence Olivier, Richard Burton, John Gielgud, and now . . . Hildy Muldman?* Elizabeth laughed bitterly at the idea.

Hildy's insults echoed in her mind. *Maybe Hildy should write a play and call it* Memoirs of a Talentless Thespian, she mused, grimacing. *She's incorrigible—how could she have made that "Semitalented Bore" crack in front of Vince?* Elizabeth's eyes regained their familiar sparkle as she recalled Vince's supportive words. *He almost makes putting up with the Muldman monster . . . OK,* she thought with a smile as she ran her hand over the plush velvet of a chair.

Elizabeth's smile disappeared as her thoughts drifted back to Hildy. *Vince is right—her insults aren't worth the bother,* she told herself, shrugging. *I have more important things to concentrate on— like how I'm going to get a performance out of her! But first I'm going home and taking a bath. Maybe Tish has an aromatherapy antidote for an overdose of Hildy Muldman.*

She had walked out of the theater and started

heading toward the subway when her eye was caught by a bedraggled vagrant on the other side of the street. "Tom?" Elizabeth gasped in disbelief.

"You don't know how happy I am to see you!" Tom cried as he shambled across the street. He thrust a soggy bunch of daisies in her face.

"What happened?" Elizabeth demanded, shocked by his appearance. Her eyes widened as she noticed the mud-splashed trousers, broken shoes, and mustard stains that combined to transform Tom from a handsome young professional into a disreputable-looking bum.

"This city is a jungle, Elizabeth," he began breathlessly. "You have no idea! I thought body piercing was horrible, but Krull was perfectly *nice* compared to some of the people I've met! How was I supposed to know that Slimehog was related to Unnatural Man? Or that drag queens can make chicken potpies? Should I just give up and write for the poodle paper?" He buried his head on her shoulder. "Oh, Liz, I feel so *lost!*"

OK, where did Tom leave his mind? Elizabeth wondered as she stroked Tom's hair calmly. *Is this some bizarre aftereffect of the stress-relieving treatment?*

"I'm sorry," Tom mumbled. "I never thought I'd be in this position. I was so sure that I would just land a sweet job once I got here. Who knew that it would be so tough?" He lifted his head and stared into Elizabeth's eyes like a lost puppy.

"It's all right, Tom," Elizabeth said with more compassion than she felt. *But I'm too tired to deal with this right now,* she added silently. *Besides, this has been going on* all week! *How hard could it be to get an internship in a city this big?*

Guilt seeping into her veins, Elizabeth shifted her books, took Tom by the arm, and headed west. "Tell you what," she began. "Why don't you let me treat us to a nice dinner?" She stole a side-long glance at her boyfriend, wondering if he was presentable enough to be allowed inside a restaurant. She was *not* relieved to see that he looked even worse than she had thought.

Tom leaned against her as if he had forgotten how to walk. "Liz, you're a lifesaver," he said with a sigh, his voice overflowing with gratitude.

"Well . . . there are lots of great places on Restaurant Row," Elizabeth suggested, referring to the nearby cluster of well-known theatrical hangouts. *Those places are probably used to serving flaky actors,* she reasoned, *so Tom won't stand out too much.*

Her train of thought was interrupted by a persistent slapping sound on the pavement. She stopped walking and motioned for Tom to do the same. The noise stopped abruptly. As soon as they moved forward it began again. "I think someone's following us," Elizabeth whispered, too frightened to turn around.

"Following us?" Tom's brow wrinkled in confusion. "Oh! Sorry, that's just my broken shoe flapping on the pavement."

"Poor Tom," Elizabeth murmured, but she couldn't help feeling a small twinge. *What if Tom never gets a job?* she wondered anxiously. *What if he's this down-and-out the whole summer?*

"You know, Elizabeth, I was thinking," Tom began. "Since I don't have any work, I'm completely free all day tomorrow. If you want, I could come to the theater with you and watch you work. Wouldn't that be nice?"

Elizabeth's eyes widened in alarm. "Sure, Tom . . . that would be . . . great." She squeezed his arm with one hand and crossed her fingers with the other.

"Even cleaning out the toilets wasn't as humiliating as this," Jessica muttered grimly as she scrubbed the floor of Pruitt's office on her hands and knees. "At least then I had Bev, Sunshine, and Annette to keep me company."

She winced as she spilled some soapy water on her hands. "Jeez, my hands will be *wrecked* by the end of the summer," Jessica moaned. "What will Izzy say the next time we have a manicure session at Theta house?" She hung her head in shame as she finished the last of the floor.

Jessica let out a long, slow breath. "OK, what now?" she asked herself. She sat back on her heels and pushed a strand of blond hair out of her face. *This place looks perfectly clean to me,* she thought. *In fact, it looks too clean. There's no personality! And the decor . . .* Jessica suppressed a shudder. *I figured the evil drillmaster would at least have* bad *taste. I didn't think she'd have* no *taste at all!*

Pruitt's office looked even more depressing and institutional than the rest of the quarters at FSSA. The walls were painted a moldy green, and the floor was stained old cinder block. The only light in the room came from a harsh, naked lightbulb and a window so tiny it was downright sad. The furniture, consisting of an old file cabinet, a huge battered metal desk, and a matching chair, did nothing to liven up the place.

"This room doesn't have to be that bad," Jessica mused, mentally redecorating. She squinted, picturing how the room would look with some bright posters and a few knickknacks scattered around. *Maybe a straw basket of potpourri, a pretty mug with pencils. She could put all those papers away in the drawers. . . .*

Jessica sat bolt upright, her eyes sparkling with enthusiasm. The first real smile she'd had in days lit up her face. *Well, well. Hello, drawers!* she thought gleefully. *Let's see what nasty little secrets Pruitt has hidden away, shall we?*

Jessica skipped over to the desk. *Hmmm, where to start?* she wondered, lowering herself into the cold metal chair and eagerly reaching for the top drawer.

"Curses! Locked!" Jessica cried out in irritation. She tested each of the drawers, but her frustration grew when none of them gave way.

What about this one? she wondered, pulling on the center drawer. Jessica went flying backward as the drawer came free in her hand. *Bingo!* Jessica gleefully began rooting around. "Let's see . . . a roll of Life Savers." She popped one of the candies in her mouth. "Breathtaking! OK, there's a package of stickies, some paper clips—what, no *hand lotion?*—an old eraser. . . . I don't believe it!" Jessica sat back, shocked. "I guess it figures; someone as dull and boring as Pruitt can't *possibly* have any juicy secrets."

Jessica propped her boots up on the desk and sighed. She racked her brain, wondering how she could help make Pruitt's life a little more miserable. "I've got it!" Jessica cried. She lunged forward and began scrabbling in the drawer. "I'll superglue Pruitt's bony butt to the chair!"

As she rummaged around for the tube she'd sworn had been there just seconds before, her nimble fingers brushed by a small metal object taped to the back of the drawer. "Whoa! What's this?" She carefully felt its outline. "A key?" Jessica quirked her eyebrows. "Now what would sweet little Pruitt be doing with a mysterious key hidden away in her drawer?"

Jessica gasped as leaden steps suddenly echoed down the hall. "Pruitt!" she hissed, quickly slamming the drawer shut. She had just enough time to stand at attention before old Pruneface came barging in.

"All right, princess, let's see if you managed to carry out *this* assignment to satisfaction." Pruitt gave Jessica a withering look as she donned a pair of white gloves and took out a magnifying glass. "The floor is disgusting," she announced, crouching down and studying it through the lens of the magnifying glass.

Who does she think she is, Sherlock Holmes? Jessica wondered with a smirk.

Pruitt pounced on the desk chair and rode it over to the window. She stood on it and swiped her white gloved forefinger across the windowsill. It came away black. "Aha! Just as I thought. You're as incompetent with a dust rag as you are with everything else!" She climbed down from the chair and stalked over to Jessica. "You're a loser," she growled, her mud-colored eyes shooting sparks. "I don't even know why I bother trying to whip you into shape. It must just be out of the goodness of my heart."

Jessica noticed that Pruitt had flecks of green stuff in between her teeth, and she bit the inside of her cheek to keep from laughing.

"I'll give you one more chance, princess. I want you to come back and *really* clean this place.

Tomorrow." A cruel smile slowly spread across her face. *"During dinner."* Pruitt peeled off her gloves and tossed them at Jessica before stomping out of the office.

You think that bothers me? Jessica asked silently as she tossed her golden braid over her shoulder defiantly. *I can't* wait *to come back tomorrow. I'm sure the mystery behind that key is a lot more delicious than anything they'll be serving in the mess hall!*

Elizabeth leaned back against the banquette, happiness washing over her in warm waves. Although she'd thought that taking Tom out to dinner would cheer *him* up, the elegant restaurant was acting as a balm to her own frayed nerves.

The cast and crew at the Maxwell had raved about La Bonbonnière. It was reputed not only to serve delicious food but to be one of the most popular theater hangouts in town. Elizabeth didn't know of any other place in the neighborhood, and she'd been more than a little nervous about showing up at a fancy establishment with Tom looking so ragged. Still, the maitre d' had been courtesy personified as he escorted them to a cozy corner table hidden away from the other diners.

Fully relaxed, Elizabeth sank down into the lushly upholstered seat and surveyed the room. Autographed photos of famous actors adorned the walls, and show tunes, provided by a pianist, floated throughout. The lighting was soft and romantic, and the perfume from the exquisite fresh floral bouquets was intoxicating.

Truly incredible, Elizabeth thought, her eyes widening as she looked around at the glittery New York theater crowd. *Wait—isn't that Jack Simona?* She was sure she recognized the famous theater critic seated at an adjacent table. *I wonder what he would think of my play?* she wondered, feeling a trifle queasy. The critic was well-known for his scathing reviews. *Well, I won't think about that now. I'm determined to have a good time!*

Elizabeth turned her attention to the sumptuous menu. Every possible cuisine was represented, and she had a hard time making up her mind. *The crab cakes look good. Maybe Tom and I can split— whoops, no, he's allergic to crab.* She peeked at Tom over the top of her menu. The soft candlelight bathed Tom's almost healed face in a flattering glow, and Elizabeth could hardly make out the mustard stains on his tie.

"What would you like, Tom?" Elizabeth asked gently as the waiter arrived.

"I'll have a tossed salad and the salmon with pineapple salsa." Tom handed the waiter his menu.

"I think I'll start with a salad too, and then linguine with basil and shrimp." Elizabeth smiled at the waiter, who bowed slightly and departed.

"So how was your day?" Tom asked.

"Probably not much better than yours," Elizabeth admitted with a shrug. She unfolded her linen napkin and spread it on her lap. "I think that I had a lot of illusions about how easy it would be to direct a play. Maybe I should just stick to journalism."

Tom barked out a sarcastic laugh. "That's a good one. It's not so easy to land a news job in this town." He lifted his crystal goblet of water and gulped half of it down.

"I'm sorry, Tom," Elizabeth whispered, her eyes filling with pity. She dipped her napkin in her water glass and leaned across the table to dab at some of the stains on his tie. "I guess New York is just a hard town. Things seemed so much simpler back in Sweet Valley." Elizabeth stopped dabbing and dropped her napkin on the table with a sigh. "I only hope that Jessica is having an easier time than we are."

"What are you worried about Jessica for?" Tom raised an eyebrow. "She usually manages to land on top of things and even get a little shopping done along the way."

"She *is* my twin," Elizabeth snapped. "*I* don't think it's so strange for me to be a little concerned! Why do you always feel the need to say things like that about my sister?"

"Sorry." Tom lowered his eyes. "But think about how she's spending her summer, Liz. It's a little crazy. Rewind to a few months ago, and you *know* the idea never would have crossed her mind. That's Jessica through and through."

"You don't have to tell *me* that, Tom. But that's totally beside the point. And anyway," she continued, unwilling to let the matter drop, "the last few times I've spoken to Jessica, she said some things that worried me."

"Like what?" Tom asked as he reached for the bread basket and began thickly buttering a slice of rosemary focaccia.

"She mentioned that she was having some trouble with her drill sergeant—"

Tom nearly choked on a mouthful of bread. "Jessica's probably ticked off because her sergeant won't let her sleep late or something like that," he said with his mouth full. "I hate to tell you, Elizabeth, but my sympathies are entirely with the drill sergeant."

"Stop it, Tom," Elizabeth said slowly, her forehead creased with anxiety. "From what Jessica said, this Sergeant Pruitt sounds like a real—"

"Elizabeth, is that you?" a deep, rich voice interrupted her. "I didn't know you ate here!"

Startled, Elizabeth looked up into the gorgeous face of Vince Klee. His leather jacket contrasted sharply with his self-described "pretty boy" features, lending him a dangerous quality. *Boy, he looks sexier than ever,* Elizabeth thought, her eyes briefly darting over to Tom's embarrassingly crumpled navy sport coat. *How can he wear that jacket in this heat without collapsing?*

"Vince! It's *so* nice to run into you!" Elizabeth's face lit up in a smile. "Do you already have a table, or do you want to join us?" She patted the banquette beside her.

"Thanks, don't mind if I do. My table won't be ready for a few minutes. I'm meeting my agent, but she's running a little late, and I don't feel like hanging by myself at the bar." Vince sat down beside Elizabeth, stretched out his legs, and rested one leather-clad arm against the back of the banquette, where it just touched Elizabeth's shining hair.

"Tom, I'd like you to meet Vince, the one nice guy at the Maxwell," she said smoothly. "Vince, this is my boyfriend, Tom."

"Hey." Vince nodded at Tom and then turned his attention back to Elizabeth. "I'm actually really glad that I ran into you. There's something I wanted to tell you."

"What's that?" she asked, riveted.

"I'm going to be leaving Claire's play," Vince began. "I can't take all the games she's playing. Besides, I was just offered a really plum role on a sitcom. That's why I'm meeting my agent tonight—we have to work out the terms."

Elizabeth felt as if she had just been crushed. "You can't leave, Vince!" she choked out. "You're the only one at the theater I get along with! Who else can I laugh at Hildy with?"

"I'm sure you'll find someone." Vince smiled warmly as he tucked a stray curl back into Elizabeth's ponytail. "Believe me, I'm going to miss you too. Look." He reached into his back pocket, drew out a card, and scribbled down several numbers. "That's my agent's phone number, my cell phone number, and my home number. I want you to call me as soon as you get back to California, OK? I can't wait to hear how everything turned out."

"Vince!" a dark-haired woman in a Chanel suit called from across the room.

"Hey, there's my agent—I've got to run." Vince stood up and kissed Elizabeth on the forehead. "Keep in touch," he said softly. "Nice meeting you," he told Tom, shaking his hand. And as suddenly as he had arrived, he was gone.

Chapter Six

Well, what a surprise! Tom fumed silently. *My girlfriend, who clearly thinks I've turned into a loser, has been spending her days with a guy who looks like Mr. America, only better!* Tom glowered at Vince Klee's retreating back. *Who's he kidding with that leather jacket anyway? I hate it when guys who earn a gazillion dollars try and look down-and-out.*

He surreptitiously rubbed his hand, which was still throbbing from the iron strength of Vince's grip. Tom had always been pretty satisfied with his build; he used to be the starting quarterback for the SVU football team, after all. But Tom knew he couldn't compete with the rippled, sculpted biceps and shoulders that had been threatening to burst the seams of Vince's jacket. *What, does the guy bench-press in his sleep?* Tom wondered, scowling.

"Isn't he sweet?" Elizabeth enthused.

"Yeah, real sweet," Tom grunted. He couldn't

help but notice how his girlfriend suddenly looked the sunniest she'd looked all evening. *Clearly Vince has a positive effect on her,* he noted darkly. *Oh, well, at least Mr. Studly Buff-Bod's going back to California.* Tom smiled smugly until his reflection in the Venetian mirror above the banquette made him do a double take.

I look like I've been hit by a truck! he realized with a gasp. *No, I look like I've been through a world war! No, I look worse than Krull!* His hair looked as if it hadn't been washed for the past month, and his clothes appeared to have been slept in for the past decade. *No wonder Elizabeth brightened up like that. Pop quiz, which would a totally perfect girl like Elizabeth Wakefield prefer? A gorgeous movie star who makes a mint of money or a college guy who looks like a bum and can't get a job to save his life?*

"It was nice of him to give me all his phone numbers, don't you think?" Elizabeth continued brightly.

"Oh, sure," Tom mumbled. "Why didn't he give you his car phone number too? Or what about the special extension he probably has in his shower?"

"Excuse me?" Elizabeth asked as she began picking at the salad the waiter had placed before her. "I didn't catch what you just said." After Tom refused to answer, she sighed. "I'm really going to miss Vince," she breathed, clearly oblivious to the havoc she was wreaking with Tom's heart.

I bet she's going to miss him! he thought viciously. *Well, at least he'll be out of town for the rest of the summer—but wait a minute, doesn't absence make the heart grow fonder?* Tom dug into his salad with as much disgust as if it were dog food.

"Is anything wrong, Tom?" Elizabeth asked. She gestured with her fork toward his dish. "You don't seem to be enjoying your salad."

"Nothing's wrong," Tom said in a funereal tone. When the smile faded from Elizabeth's face, Tom kicked himself under the table. *Some boyfriend you are,* he chastised himself. *Your girlfriend takes you to a great restaurant, and all you can do is feel* bad!

Tom returned to his salad with a grin plastered on his face. *Enough with feeling sorry for myself,* he vowed. *I'm going out tomorrow and getting a job. A great job. And I'll make Elizabeth respect me. In fact, she'll be so in awe of me that she won't even be able to remember Vince . . . whatever his name is!*

This is so romantic, Elizabeth thought as she and Tom walked home slowly, hand in hand, along the tree-lined boulevard of Riverside Drive. After the frantic pace of the theater district it was soothing to hear the summer breeze rustling through the leaves and to see the sparkle of lights reflected in the Hudson River.

Dinner was fantastic, Elizabeth thought,

gazing out over the water. *And now I'm walking with the man I love in one of the greatest cities in the world. . . . So why do I feel sad?* She sighed as the breeze ruffled her hair and stirred the soft tendrils that framed her face.

Elizabeth gazed at Tom, his handsome, strong profile silhouetted in the moonlight, and her heart fluttered. *What's wrong with me?* Elizabeth asked herself, a slight frown marring her lovely face. *I love Tom. Why should I care if Vince goes back to California?*

But she *did* care; there was no use pretending otherwise. Having Vince around had been the one thing that made rehearsals at the Maxwell bearable. Elizabeth closed her eyes briefly as a vision of Hildy Muldman limping about the stage flashed before her eyes. *Vince was the only person there who could make me laugh,* she thought, biting her lip. *I need all the comic relief I can get—and the support too. What's going to happen the next time Hildy insults me? Will I blow up? Burst into tears? At least Vince was there to keep my emotions in check.* Of course, she couldn't deny that his taking her hand had been a nice bonus. His touch was so warm and nurturing—

"Here we are," Tom announced as they reached the entrance to Tish's building. While the building was just as beautiful as the others along Riverside Drive, it was one of the few without a doorman; Tom took out a borrowed set of keys and let Elizabeth inside. He followed, his broken heel making scuffing noises on the black-and-white marble checkerboard floor as they made their way across the lobby.

"Thanks for dinner, Liz," Tom said softly. "I had a great time."

"It was my pleasure." Elizabeth smiled at Tom warmly, but she couldn't stop worrying about what the next day's rehearsal would bring. Stepping into the small, mahogany-lined elevator, she punched the button to Tish's floor after Tom closed the accordion-style door.

"Um," Elizabeth murmured, surprised as Tom's arms came around her in a crushing hug. The feeling of strength that flowed from his body was delicious. *Have I been ignoring Tom tonight?* Elizabeth wondered with an uncomfortable twinge. "What's that for?" she asked teasingly as she gazed into his deep brown eyes.

"For being the best girlfriend in the world," Tom said huskily, his arms still holding hers in a loose embrace.

I'm being silly about Vince, Elizabeth thought, resting her head against Tom's chest. *So OK, maybe I won't have anyone to laugh with at rehearsals, but I still get to come home to a wonderful boyfriend.*

The elevator arrived, and they stepped off into the vestibule. After Tom opened the door for her, she inhaled deeply as they entered the apartment.

"Mmm, smells like Tish is baking something wonderful." Elizabeth sniffed the air appreciatively. "I think it's gingerbread." She put her books down on the ivory inlaid console table that was home to a figurine of a Cretan goddess.

"Tish?" Elizabeth called, craning her head around the L shape of the living room to see if Tish was in the kitchen.

"In here, dear." Tish beckoned with one hand as she held the phone with another. The laugh lines around her eyes and mouth crinkled as she beamed sweetly. "Hold on one second; she just walked in," she said into the receiver before holding it out. "Elizabeth, your sister is on the phone."

Elizabeth's stomach dropped as she crossed the living room in two strides to grab the phone. *What is Jessica calling me about at this hour?* she wondered anxiously. "Jess?"

"Elizabeth?" Jessica's voice, more familiar to her than her own, crackled through the phone wires. Elizabeth swallowed a lump in her throat as she was overwhelmed by a flood of emotion. The nonstop hustle of the past four days in New York had blurred the pain of missing her sister, but now it all came back in a rush. *Nobody can really understand what it's like to have an identical twin,* Elizabeth thought mistily.

"Jess? I'm here; what's up?" *Please let it be that she found some great new bikinis in a mall down there!* Elizabeth prayed silently. She pulled up a cheerfully painted stool to one of the counters and began spooning into the bowl of gingerbread batter.

"Do you know any good books on boxing technique? My punch needs to pack a little more power, but I think my footwork's pretty good. After all, the latest dances *do* incorporate elements of the martial arts, and I did go to some really cutting edge clubs before I left Sweet Valley. . . ."

What is Jess going on about? Elizabeth wondered, baffled, as her sister rambled on. She was able to catch only about one word in five, but the words she did catch made her blood run cold. *Boxing technique? Footwork? This sounds even worse than I imagined!*

"Jess, slow down." Elizabeth pushed the stool away and paced back and forth across the blue-and-white-tiled floor. "Could you tell me exactly what is going on?"

"Well, the thing is, I kind of have a little tiny problem, Elizabeth."

Jessica never has little tiny *problems,* Elizabeth thought, frozen in place. The spoon that she had been using to scrape the bowl clattered to the floor. "What is it, Jess?" Elizabeth asked, struggling to keep her voice calm and even.

"It wouldn't be so bad, really." Jessica sounded like she was trying to convince herself as well as Elizabeth. "I mean, I *am* pretty hard to beat, in every sense of the word. . . ."

Elizabeth couldn't help smiling at her sister's

comment, but Jessica's remarks were doing nothing to quell her anxiety.

"But Pruitt is a Golden Gloves boxer!" she continued. "Can you handle it? I should have known. I mean, she looks like an award-winning freak, so it's not surprising that she actually *is* one. You should have seen her in the gym today, Elizabeth! She knocked out this guy that looked like Arnold Schwarzenegger's bigger brother!"

When Jessica paused to take a breath, Elizabeth tried to make sense of her sister's confused monologue. "Let me get this straight, Jess. You're going to *fight* this creep Pruitt that you've been complaining about? And—" Elizabeth put her hand on the counter to steady herself. "And she's a Golden Gloves boxer? Did I get that right?"

"Yes," Jessica said meekly.

"Jessica, I just have one question for you, OK?" Elizabeth began through gritted teeth. "Did you get a case of sunstroke? Is that it? Because the only other explanation I can come up with for your doing something like this is that you've gone completely stark raving mad!"

"I don't have sunstroke. Maybe I'm a little burned—that witch Pruitt confiscated my sunblock, you know. In fact, I think my nose is starting to peel! Do you think you could send me some aloe? That should help. I know that when Lila Fowler went to this one salon in Paris after she'd taken a cruise to Antigua—"

"Jessica!" Elizabeth interrupted. "I want to *save* your skin, not make sure it's moisturized! You *have* to get out of that fight! Do you hear me, Jessica? You have to quit—or you'll get yourself killed!"

"But Elizabeth, I just can't *quit!*" Jessica shrieked into the receiver. Quickly she looked around to make sure that Pruitt wasn't snooping somewhere nearby. *Although knowing Pruitt, she probably has spies all over the place,* Jessica told herself. She closed the door of the phone booth tightly and crammed herself as far back in the corner as possible. The result of this maneuver was that one of Jessica's shoulders was up around her ear and the other one was twisted behind her back. But she didn't care; besides, the pain would probably help her build up tolerance for Saturday night.

"*Why* can't you quit, Jessica?"

Jessica had a mental image of her sister standing with her hands on her hips, her face set in a scowl. It was a look Jessica knew well. She'd seen it enough times over the past eighteen years. It was the kind of look she got when she borrowed Elizabeth's silk blouse and got ketchup on it. It was the kind of look she got when she messed up Elizabeth's side of the room they shared in Dickenson Hall at SVU. Jessica had thought that she hated it when Elizabeth scolded her over petty things. But the truth was, there was nothing that would have made Jessica happier at the moment than to wake up in Sweet Valley and have Elizabeth bugging her to do the laundry.

Blinking back the hot tears that were pricking her eyelids, Jessica continued. "Don't you get it?" she begged in disbelief. "If I quit, I'll lose everyone's respect! Besides, I don't feel like seeing the gloating look on Pruitt's face when I announce that I'm giving up. It'll probably make me puke."

Jessica held the phone away to protect her eardrums as Elizabeth's voice came screeching down the line, but there wasn't enough room in the booth to escape the righteous blaze of Elizabeth's words.

"Excuse me? Oh, of course, I understand *now*. That makes *perfect* sense. You'd rather have your front teeth knocked out than see the expression on Pruitt's face!"

Well, I suppose that does *sound pretty lame,* Jessica admitted silently as she clutched the phone. "It's not that simple, Liz," she said with a sigh as she returned the receiver to her ear. But at this point she knew there was no way she could make her sister see her side of things. *I'll just say goodbye,* Jessica decided. Swallowing hard, she wondered if this would be the last time she would ever bid her sister farewell.

"Listen, I have to go." Jessica sniffled. "If you can think of anything to help me out . . . give me a call. Bye, Elizabeth." She choked back a sob. "You've been a great sister." She replaced the receiver gently on its hook and proceeded to unwedge herself from the phone booth.

Jessica slumped dejectedly down the narrow hall back to the barracks. Her conversation with Elizabeth hadn't cheered her up the way she had hoped. *Well, what did you expect?* she asked herself. *That Elizabeth would just wave a magic wand and make everything better?* Jessica sighed bitterly. The fact was, she *had* been hoping just that.

Even worse, her brief sojourn in the phone booth seemed to be having lingering effects. Jessica could hardly stand up straight, and her uneven progress down the hall was strikingly reminiscent of the Hunchback of Notre Dame. *So much for my posture,* she lamented. *I'm sure Pruitt will give me ten demerits at inspection later!*

Jessica entered the barracks and flung herself facedown on her bed.

"Don't worry, Jessica." Sunshine swung her head down from her perch on the top bunk. Her copper-colored hair hung in ribbons over the edge. "Everything will work out." She reached down to pat Jessica on the shoulder.

Jessica rolled over on her back, clutching the pillow to her chest. She looked up at Sunshine, grateful for the kind words, but she could see the fear that lurked behind Sunshine's eyes. *Who's she kidding?* she wondered incredulously. *We both know I'm dead!*

"Yeah, Jessica, don't sweat it. You'll toast her," Bev called out from her bunk, but her words didn't carry a lot of conviction.

Jessica could feel the anxiety that radiated from the other girls in the room. Annette was barely able to smile, and none of her barrack mates could seem to meet Jessica's eyes.

Of course they're anxious! Jessica told herself, staring at a crack on the bottom of Sunshine's top bunk. *I'd be worried too if I knew I was going to have a corpse on my hands!*

Jessica pounded her forehead in frustration. *Come on, think! You've been in tough situations before and survived! You just need to . . .*

Wait a minute! Jessica sat bolt upright, her mind working furiously, the beginnings of a smile tugging at the corners of her mouth.

I've got it! That key in Pruitt's desk . . . once I find out what it's protecting, I can expose Pruneface and get her locked up in stocks before the fight ever happens! Jessica resolved, nearly giddy with relief. *After all, there's nobody who can snoop and pry better than yours truly!*

With a triumphant smile on her face and her salvation at hand, Jessica fell back on her bunk and squeezed her pillow with joy.

Chapter
Seven

Who would have believed that directing an off-Broadway play and gum surgery would have so much in common? Elizabeth asked herself as she climbed out of the subway and hurried across Seventh Avenue to the Maxwell Theater.

Oh, c'mon, gum surgery isn't that bad, she thought, adjusting her baseball cap against the Friday morning sun. *At least you get Novocain! Now that Vince is gone, there won't be anything to take the pain away.* Elizabeth winced just thinking about it.

Maybe if I play it cool and go along with Hildy's games, she'll start to listen to my ideas more seriously, Elizabeth thought, frowning. *We're both adults. We should be able to come to some sort of compromise—*

"Hey, beautiful, how come so sad?" a seductive voice murmured at her elbow.

Elizabeth looked up, startled. "Vince!" she

cried, her frown instantly replaced by a wide smile.

Vince grinned back, his eyes crinkling in the sun. "Surprised to see me?"

"I sure am," Elizabeth said. "What are you doing here?" She gestured toward the Maxwell. "I thought you were already on your way back to California!"

Vince shrugged, a chagrined expression on his face. "I thought so too until this morning. Look." He unrolled a glossy magazine that had been tucked under his arm and began flipping through the pages.

"What's that?"

"This? This is *The Hollywood Page*," Vince said. "You've never seen it? It's one of the most important publications in the industry. Actors kill to get good press in here. And if they get bad press, *brrr . . .*" Vince shuddered theatrically. "Anyway, read this and weep." He folded back a page and thrust the magazine into Elizabeth's hands.

Poor Vince—the magazine must have slammed him! Elizabeth thought sympathetically as she studied the article. A large shot of Vince, his shirt unbuttoned and his hair windblown, dominated the left side of the page. *It's so hard to believe that's the same person,* Elizabeth thought as she quickly scanned the caption underneath: *Vince Klee, one of the most talented young actors in Hollywood today, demonstrates his commitment to his craft by treading the boards.*

"But Vince." Elizabeth looked up, confusion written on her face. "What's the problem? This sounds like great press."

"Keep going," Vince urged.

Elizabeth turned her attention back to the magazine.

Few film actors have the discipline necessary to take on the demands of the stage. Vince Klee, however, proves himself to be a different breed than the rest of his brat pack colleagues. Mr. Klee is spending his summer in New York, where he is lending his name and considerable talents to champion the work of an unknown playwright, Claire Sterling. If only more actors would show this kind of dedication to their art, perhaps the theater would come back to life. . . .

"Vince, this is incredible!" she enthused. "If it were any more positive, it would be a eulogy." Elizabeth's eyes sparkled with happiness as she handed back the magazine. "This should really help you kick off that new sitcom you were talking about."

"Don't you see, Elizabeth?" Vince groaned as he leaned back against the stage door entrance. "I'm stuck! How can I quit now after a write-up like this?" He ran his hands through his hair distractedly. "My agent called me this morning, practically freaking out. She says that if I leave the play for a sitcom, *The Hollywood Page* will have my blood all over the next issue." Vince laughed bitterly as he met Elizabeth's gaze with grave seriousness. "She was pretty upset about losing the commission on the sitcom, but I'm stuck here, like it or not." He shook his hands frantically in frustration.

"Oh, Vince, I'm really sorry," Elizabeth whispered sympathetically.

"You know . . . I was hoping you could help me figure something out."

"I'd love to, Vince, but what can I possibly do?"

"I was hoping you could think of some scheme to get me fired—you know, help me come up with something outrageous that would be sure to get me the boot."

Elizabeth threw back her head and laughed. *Boy, does Vince have the wrong Wakefield twin!* she thought. "Sorry, Vince," Elizabeth said. "I'd help you if I could, but as far as I'm concerned, if Hildy's antics and Claire's insisting on nudity haven't gotten *them* fired, then nothing's outrageous enough."

"I guess you're right," Vince agreed. "In fact, if I did do something really wacky, Claire would probably think it was some new theatrical concept and incorporate it in the play." He shook his head with a sigh. "Oh, well, looks like you won't be getting rid of me so easily, Elizabeth." Vince nudged the backstage door open with his shoulder.

"I'm glad," Elizabeth admitted with a coy

smile as she followed him inside and blinked to adjust to the darkness of the theater. While she knew Vince was miserable about his situation, she couldn't help but be buoyed by excitement that they wouldn't be separated so soon. But her heart sank instantly when Hildy sashayed past.

"Oh, look, it's the two true *romantics* of the theater," she drawled snidely, looking more bizarre than ever. She was decked out in a pair of baggy pants hitched up with a man's tie and a tattered vest several sizes too big. A green felt hat perched jauntily on her frizzy hair completed the costume.

With a sigh Elizabeth waved good-bye to Vince and headed to her rehearsal room, preparing for the first battle of the day.

"So you see, I *do* have quite a bit of journalistic experience." Tom fingered his tie nervously. "I'm also good with technical equipment. I know how to edit, do film-to-video transfer, and sound mixing."

Tom had woken up filled with resolve that he would land a job before the weekend. Tish had helped him get his clothes in order, and by the time Tom left the house with his suit freshly pressed, a clean tie, and a new pair of shoes, he felt ready to take on the world. His positive attitude was fading quickly, however, underneath the steely glance that Wilson W. Kroop, head of the Acme

Employment Agency, was leveling at him. His dead, insectlike eyes studied Tom for a second too long before he extended his hand to take Tom's resume.

Maybe this wasn't such a good idea after all, Tom thought, resisting the urge to loosen his tie. *Maybe I should keep trying to find a cushy job on my own.* Right now the only positive thing about his decision to try Acme seemed to be that the place was air-conditioned. Tom was beginning to suspect, with heavy heart, that a cushy job—at least as procured by Mr. Kroop—was *not* in his immediate future.

Well, at least this place doesn't smell like kitty litter, Tom thought as he took a deep breath of the canned office air. But he had to admit that while the Acme offices *were* clean, they were also a monument to bad taste. The walls were covered in a series of hideous modern art prints. Tom couldn't make out if they were of the Brooklyn Bridge at sunset or of the polar bears in the Bronx Zoo. The carpet was a mass of orange-and-lime-colored swirls, and the furniture looked like it had been given away free with a full tank of gas. Tom tore his gaze away from trying to decipher the prints and looked with fading hope at Mr. Kroop as he perused Tom's resume.

Mr. Kroop adjusted his horn-rimmed glasses and ran a hand across the two hairs that covered his shiny pink scalp. He held Tom's resume between his thumb and forefinger as if it were a used handkerchief.

"Hmm, yes, *campus* television station, *high-school* paper. Yes, Mr. Warts—"

"Watts," Tom corrected him. He tapped his feet in irritation on the green-and-orange carpet.

"I can see that you have experience," Wilson W. Kroop went on smoothly. He said *experience* as if it were some kind of disease. "But you see, Mr. Witts—"

"Watts."

"Yes." Mr. Kroop cleared his throat. "You see, we have people with *network* television experience coming in here. We have people who've worked on *professional* papers. And as for technical experience, well, Mr. Wetts—"

"Watts." Tom struggled to keep from strangling Mr. Kroop with his yellow-and-purple-striped tie.

"Yes, well, as I was saying, we have people here who have worked in film production for major studios." He glanced at Tom's resume once more. "I'm sorry, but I'm afraid your *experience* just isn't up to the standard that we usually look at. What's this—*Young Journalists' Citation for Excellence?*" His laugh sounded like a frog croaking. "Really, Mr. Welts, we have *Pulitzer Prize* winners in here." He shook his head sorrowfully as he handed Tom's resume back to him.

Yeah, right, as if a Pulitzer winner would even

give this guy the time of day! Tom thought indignantly. *The guy doesn't have to stand up and cheer over my resume, but did he have to be so patronizing?* "Thanks anyway," Tom said morosely as he stood, gathered up his briefcase, and prepared to leave.

"May I give you a word of advice?" Mr. Kroop asked.

Tom paused with his hand on the door handle and turned around expectantly.

"I really don't think you have what it takes to make it in this town. Perhaps you should just go back to Sweet Meadows." Mr. Kroop smiled, revealing capped teeth that had probably looked great forty years earlier.

Enraged, Tom narrowed his eyes and breathed fire. "Listen, Mr. *Kreep*," he seethed. "I didn't come here for your two-bit advice. I came here for a job, Mr. *Krock*. Obviously you don't have the resources to help me." Tom was gratified to see the employment officer flinch under the acid dripping from his voice. "So don't give me any nonsense about Pulitzer Prize winners because you know I'm the best thing you've seen all day, Mr. *Karp!*" Tom punctuated his final words by slamming the door to the office so hard that it rattled on its hinges. He marched quickly through the waiting room into the stairwell, flying down the stairs and bursting out the fire door into the lobby.

Wham! Coffee cups went flying, and Tom

flung his arms out to keep himself from falling as he collided with a young woman holding a deli box.

"I'm really sorry," Tom apologized as he bent to help the young woman pick up the sodden mess. "It was an accident—"

"This is the last straw!" she muttered angrily, shaking droplets of coffee out of her mass of auburn curls. "I'm quitting this lousy job!"

Tom pricked up his ears. "Job? What job? You're quitting a *job?*"

"Yeah, I'm a production assistant, but not any longer!" She kicked one of the paper coffee cups savagely. "I've had it with *Tease-n-Tell!*"

Now why does that name sound so familiar? Tom asked himself. *Of course!* He snapped his fingers in recognition. *It's that sleaze-'em and please-'em show I was stuck watching at Tish's on Tuesday. What was the topic? "Surprise, Mom, I'm a Hooker"?* Tom quirked an eyebrow. *Well, I guess my journalistic ideals are about to take a vacation!*

"So . . . ," Tom began with feigned casualness, "where does *Tease-n-Tell* broadcast from?"

"Right there." The girl jerked her thumb at a glass-fronted suite of offices across from the elevators. "I'm out of here," she proclaimed, shaking the last of the coffee out of her hair. She strode angrily out of the building and hailed a cab.

Tom looked down at the mess on the floor. *Well, well. Sometimes opportunity knocks, and sometimes it just spills coffee all over you,* he thought with a grin as he began counting the cups. "Five, six, seven . . . got it!"

Tom sprinted out the door into a nearby deli. "Seven coffees, three light, sugar on the side," he called over his shoulder to the counterman as he selected seven Danish. Peeling the last remaining bills out of his wallet and tossing them to the cashier, Tom grabbed the goodies. Making sure to hold them carefully, he walked swiftly back to the *Tease-n-Tell* offices.

Taking a deep breath, Tom paused outside the door. "Here goes," he murmured, opening the door with his foot. He headed straight past the protesting receptionist toward a group of people who were sitting around a conference table discussing a bunch of storyboards. They all looked up in surprise.

"Who are you?" a guy asked.

"I'm your new PA," Tom answered with a grin.

"I hope my friend Lila sent me some beauty products from the south of France," Jessica said as she fished in the pocket of her jumpsuit for her tiny metal mailbox key. The tiny post office was jammed as recruits piled through the door, eager to receive their care packages and love letters.

"I hope I got another letter from my boyfriend. He wrote me *three* last week." Bev flipped through a pile of envelopes.

"Boyfriend? I just hope my grandmother sent me some more cigars," Sunshine said, swinging open the door to her mailbox.

Harlan strutted by with a sneer. "Well, I don't care about cigars or boyfriends, but if the new issue of *Soldier of Fortune* didn't come, someone's going to pay."

Jessica mimed sticking a finger down her throat before she began sifting through her mail. *Let's see, no beauty products from Lila, but there's a letter from Mom and Dad, and . . . what's this? It's not even stamped.* "What now?" Jessica groaned as she recognized the pink stamp that indicated an FSSA memo.

"What is it?" Sunshine appeared at her elbow, clutching a box of Havana's finest.

"Something wrong, Jessica?" Annette asked, looking over her shoulder.

"I'm afraid to find out," Jessica admitted. "It's probably a summons from Pruitt telling me that I have swamp duty or something!"

"Go on and open it," Bev urged. "It won't improve with time."

With trembling fingers Jessica broke the seal on the envelope. "'Private Wakefield, you are hereby requested to report to my office at oh-eight-hundred hours,'" she read aloud. "This sounds like some kind of summons!" Jessica wailed, too sick to read the rest of the letter.

"Let me see that." Sunshine grabbed the sheet

of paper from Jessica. "'On Monday morning . . .' blah blah blah . . . oooh, listen to *this!*" she said excitedly. "'I have set up five separate interviews for you with various security firms, including Star Watchers.' It's signed Commander Phipps!"

"Let me see that letter!" Jessica shrieked. "I don't believe it!" She started jumping up and down. "I've read all about Star Watchers! They protect all the hottest celebs!" *Well, clearly Commander Phipps is a man with an eye for potential,* Jessica thought, preening. *Clearly Pit Bull Pruitt doesn't have the last word around here. . . .*

"Oh no," Jessica groaned. The memo fluttered to the ground, and Jessica swayed slightly, her face turning a deadly shade of white.

"What is it?" Annette held on to Jessica's elbow to prevent her from falling.

"Need some help, honey?" Harlan sidled up.

"Get lost," Bev growled. "C'mon, Jessica, let's sit you down."

"Thanks, guys," Jessica said gratefully as they led her over to a bench in the corner. Some of the slats were missing, but Jessica didn't care. "It's just that it hit me all of a sudden how much I have to lose if Pruitt creams me on Saturday." Jessica gulped. "I mean, getting in tight with a group like Star Watchers is the whole reason I came to Nowheresville! How am I going to be able to interview on Monday if Pruitt knocks me unconscious tomorrow?"

"Don't worry . . . we have a plan," Sunshine murmured in a low voice.

"What plan? What are you talking about?" Jessica looked back and forth between her bunk mates, bewildered.

"It's not exactly on the up-and-up," Annette began.

"But then neither is Pruitt," Bev finished, tossing her head defiantly.

"Well, what is it?" Jessica leaned forward eagerly, some of the color returning to her face. *Should I tell them about the hidden key?* she wondered. *Maybe that will help them with whatever they're cooking up.*

Annette looked stern. "You're much better off not knowing, Jessica."

"What's that supposed to mean?" Jessica asked, baffled. "Why shouldn't I—"

"Believe me," Sunshine interrupted. Her voice was grim, and her gaze looked threatening. "You don't want to know what's going on."

"Of course I do!" Jessica protested.

"It requires your total innocence, Jessica," Sunshine continued mysteriously. "That is, if it has any chance of working at all."

"What kind of a plan is *that?* How will I know what to do?"

"Sorry, but this is the way it has to be." Bev crossed her arms in front of her chest, and her cocoa complexion seemed to grow cloudy as she gave Jessica a look that would have withered Pruitt herself.

An icy swirl of anxiety shimmied up Jessica's spine as she took in her friend's surreptitious glances. She couldn't understand it—one minute they *seemed* like her friends, and now . . . *Well, now they seem like they have it in for me!* she realized with dread. Jessica sank back against the bench, pressing her palms to her temples where a massive headache was threatening to explode. She prayed that she was just being paranoid.

"Trust us, Jessica." Annette spoke softly, but the words carried a deadly chill.

Trust them? she asked herself incredulously. *I don't know* who *to trust. One thing's for sure—I'm glad I didn't let them in on* my *plan. It may be the only chance I have!*

"This is where we keep the office supplies—fax paper, staples, stuff like that. If you can't find anything, just yell."

"Sure," Tom replied with a smile at Ron Mullen, the *Tease-n-Tell* intern who had been showing him around the offices.

"And over here is where we get the editing done." Ron pushed open the door to the editing facilities.

Tom whistled. "Looks pretty state-of-the-art," he murmured appreciatively, taking in the shiny new equipment.

"Yeah," Ron agreed, giving Tom a friendly smile as they moved away from the editing room. "The facilities here are excellent, and a lot of the techs and other interns are first-rate. It helps to make up for the rest of it."

"The rest of what?" Tom asked in confusion.

"Well, let's just say that the stories *Tease-n-Tell* comes up with aren't the most *intellectually* stimulating." Ron smirked. "Still, the people are good, and you'll be surprised by Joey, our producer." Ron gestured toward the large corner office, where Tom could see Joey dictating through the open door. "He's a little rough around the edges but a real pro." Ron led Tom over to the cubicle that would be Tom's office. "I'm going to grab lunch. If you want to order in, there're probably some menus on your desk. The Mexican place is the best around."

"Hey, thanks for showing me the ropes," Tom called after Ron's departing figure. He grinned as he propped his feet up on the desk and leaned back in his comfortably upholstered swivel chair. He snapped open his briefcase and took out a silver framed photograph of Elizabeth. After arranging the picture of Elizabeth and loosening his tie, Tom got down to work. His smile faded slightly, however, as he studied the file that Joey, his new boss, had handed him.

"*Tease-n-Tell* isn't exactly *Meet the Press*," Tom murmured as he sifted through the production notes. The show focused exclusively on how to get the maximum shock mileage out of every story. In addition to in-studio segments such as interviews with women who ran off with their sons-in-law, there were occasional taped "news items"—exposés on everything from politicians caught with their pants down to miracle cures for cancer.

"Well, I knew I was going to have to park my journalistic integrity at the door," Tom reminded himself, his joy swiftly evaporating. "But at least I'm employed. This is better than being stuck out on the street, hustling for a job and losing Elizabeth's respect . . . Elizabeth!"

Tom hastily reached for the phone, eager to share his good news. He dialed the Maxwell, and as the actor who had picked up went to call Elizabeth to the phone, he wrote her name over and over again on a notepad.

"Tom, what's up?" Elizabeth asked. Her sweet voice sounded concerned.

She probably thinks I'm calling to tell her about the latest failed interview! Tom thought, suppressing a chuckle. "I just thought I'd let you in on one of the day's top stories," Tom drawled. "The news flash is that Tom Watts, that hot young journalist from California, is about to take the New York news scene by storm."

"Tom! You got a job! That's wonderful! I'm so happy for you! Where?"

"Uh—excuse me?" Tom's brow furrowed.

"Where are you working?" Elizabeth repeated brightly. "Is it for one of the networks?"

"The networks?" Tom's voice came out in a squeak, and he made an effort to lower it. "The networks? Well, actually . . ." He trailed off, suddenly embarrassed. *What will Elizabeth think if I tell her I'm working for Sleaze Central?* he wondered, knowing all too well how disappointed she would be at his journalistic compromise. Sweat started to form on Tom's forehead. *There's no way I can tell her,* he realized with despair.

Tom cleared his throat, stalling. His eye fell on a couple of trade journals that his predecessor had left scattered on the desk. "Classy arts programs denied funding," the cover copy shrieked. "Record number of cable newsmagazines in development this season!"

"Well, it's actually a . . . a classy cable newsmagazine currently in development." *Phew!* Tom wiped his brow in relief. *Close call, buddy!*

"That sounds exciting, Tom," Elizabeth said with enthusiasm. "If it's still in the start-up mode, they'll probably welcome a lot of input from you. I know you'll be able to come up with some really innovative concepts."

"Yeah, I'm sure," Tom said gruffly, pushing the trade journals away. "How's your day been so far?" he asked, eager to change the subject before Elizabeth asked him any more questions about his "classy cable newsmagazine" job.

"Not so bad. Well, to tell the truth, Hildy's as obnoxious as ever." Elizabeth sighed. "But Vince is staying on, and I'm so relieved because . . ."

Elizabeth continued explaining the benefits of having Vince nearby, but Tom was barely listening. His mind had shut off as soon as he heard the words *Vince* and *staying on*.

Why doesn't he go back to Hollywood where he belongs? Tom asked himself. He picked up the picture of Elizabeth and stared at it wistfully. His fingers traced her beautiful smile as he remembered the day he'd taken the photo—

". . . so because of the article, Vince is kind of stuck here," she explained.

Oh, sure, Tom thought in response, his gaze still riveted to Elizabeth's photo. *The real reason he's "stuck here" is* my girlfriend! *She's the only thing that could make a guy turn down a TV show—which is exactly what I did when I left Action 5 News!* Tom's heart sank as he envisioned Vince Klee nuzzling Elizabeth's *other* ear—the one that wasn't glued to the phone as she babbled on.

"Listen, Tom, I have to get going, OK? I can't wait to hear more about your job later. Goodbye." Elizabeth's kiss floated through the receiver.

"Bye," Tom said glumly as Elizabeth hung up. The phone dangled uselessly from his hands, emitting a sharp dial tone. Tom stared at it for a second before wrapping the cord around his neck and pretending to strangle himself.

"Arrgh," Tom cried out in frustration. "Just when I thought things were looking up—*boom*."

He hung up the phone and shook his head. "I've really dug myself into a hole this time," he muttered, burying his face in his hands. "What am I going to tell Elizabeth when she asks me about my job? She's too smart to let a lie like this past."

Tom pushed back his chair and got up to pace restlessly around his cubicle. *That's not the worst part*, a wicked voice in Tom's head reminded him. *When Elizabeth finds out you lied to her, Vince Studman will be right there to elbow you out of her life forever.*

Chapter Eight

Thank goodness Tom's doing OK, Elizabeth thought with relief. She hung up the phone and walked through the backstage area toward where Ken and Hildy were sitting on the main stage. _Now if I could just get this rehearsal under control . . ._

Elizabeth stood backstage and peered through the mass of lighting equipment to where Hildy and Ken were rehearsing. Or rather to where Ken was _sitting,_ his head in his hands, and Hildy was riding a unicycle. Elizabeth covered her mouth with her hand to hold back the fit of giggles that were threatening to erupt.

Leaning against the flats, Elizabeth struggled to compose herself. Backstage felt so alive and vibrant. The assorted props scattered around and the tech crew running back and forth with headsets created an atmosphere unlike anything Elizabeth had ever experienced. She inhaled deeply. _Ah, the smell of the_ *theater,* she mused. *Funny that all the magic should be happening back* here *while the disaster's happening onstage!* She smoothed back her hair in an effort to compose herself before she made her way out front.

"I can't take much more of this!" Ken bellowed just as Elizabeth took a seat in the front row. "I mean it!" He stood up and advanced threateningly toward Hildy, who was having trouble keeping her balance on the unicycle. Irritation radiated from his every pore, and the atmosphere onstage crackled with electricity.

Too bad Ken and Hildy can't devote that kind of energy to the play, Elizabeth thought with a sigh. "Uh, Ken, is there a problem?" she asked casually, hoping a nonconfrontational tone would help Ken to calm down.

"Problem?" Ken stared out into the houselights. "Yeah, I have a problem. I'm sharing the stage with a lunatic!" He gestured frantically toward Hildy. "Where does it say that Phoebe rides a unicycle?" He flipped through his script in a futile gesture. "I don't see anything in here about limps, unicycles, crutches, or wheelchairs!" He threw the script down on the rolltop desk, causing several of the props to roll to the floor.

"Crutches?" Hildy stopped riding and looked thoughtful. "Now *that* might actually—"

"Don't finish that sentence," Ken warned, his

tone deadly earnest. "Because if you do, I may not be responsible for my actions."

Elizabeth shook her head and waved her hands, hoping the gesture would stall Ken while she came up with a plan of action. *If I try to talk Ken down, I'll lose him,* she thought, *and besides, my sympathies are entirely with him! But if I let Hildy know that, I'll lose the only actress I have—*

"Elizabeth, I'm sorry, I really like your script, but I've had enough. I'm out of here," Ken said simply. He didn't bother looking back; he just picked up his jacket and began walking toward the exit.

"Ken, wait!" Elizabeth cried out. She hurried through the front-row aisle as fast as she could and caught up with him just as he made it to the door. "Ken, please. I know it's a really, really difficult situation, but don't just leave. Please." She put her hand placatingly on his arm. "You're really good in the part, honestly. You don't want to walk away from your first break, do you?"

Ken shrugged. "Well, *maybe* I'll show on Monday. But I'm definitely out of here for now. Don't feel bad—I know it's not *your* fault." Ken shot Hildy a dirty look before pushing open the stage door.

Elizabeth swallowed hard, fighting back tears of frustration. *I should just follow Ken right out that door and keep on going until I hit Sweet Valley,* she mused.

"Elizabeth!" Hildy trilled. "There's no need to get upset because Ken doesn't have the *artistic* maturity to understand my *vision* of the play. We don't need him." She tossed her head imperiously.

"It will be hard to get another actor at this point," Elizabeth replied sharply as she made her way back to her seat. "I just hope that Ken cools off over the weekend and decides to show up on Monday."

"Oh, Elizabeth! I hate to see you buying into such *outdated* concepts! Who needs another actor? Don't you see how much more life force this play will have if Phoebe and Gavin are played by the same performer? It will *truly* explode the myth of the weakness of the feminine half of the species."

"Could you say that again?" Elizabeth demanded, aghast, but quickly held up her hand. "No, don't!"

"I'm going to take a short break. I can see you need the rest, Elizabeth," Hildy said almost kindly. "I can understand that you're feeling slightly overwhelmed by the ingeniousness of my idea." She waltzed off the stage, clearly enchanted by her own stroke of so-called genius.

Elizabeth sat, frozen. *It doesn't matter,* she consoled herself. *I mean, who cares if my play sinks faster than the* Titanic? *There are more important things to worry about, like famine in Africa. . . .*

The sound of footsteps intruded on her

thoughts. "Ken?" she asked, turning around hopefully.

"Sorry, it's just me," Vince said as he took a seat and placed a comforting hand on her shoulder. "I heard that Ken just walked. I can't say I really blame him, but what finally pushed him over the edge?"

"Hildy wants to ride *that*." Elizabeth pointed to the stage, where the offending unicycle stood propped up against the back wall.

"She does? That's great!" Vince clapped in amusement.

"Are you *kidding*?"

"No," Vince replied with a perfectly straight face. "I think it's about time Hildy realized she was a circus act."

Elizabeth punched Vince lightly on the shoulder and collapsed into hysterical giggles. "Oh . . . thanks, Vince, I needed that. You know, I'm *so* glad you're here to cheer me up."

Vince wiped away a tear of laughter from the corner of Elizabeth's eye. "It's my pleasure," he said, smiling softly.

"Hey, Tom." Ron Mullen poked his head around the door. "Story meeting in two minutes in the conference room."

"Thanks, Ron." Tom grabbed his notebook and pens and followed Jenny Tracey, the host of *Tease-n-Tell*, as she made her way to the room where the rest of the staff was assembled. The conference area was spacious and attractive, and Tom took a second to study the stills from previous shows before he slid into one of the leather-and-chrome chairs.

At the head of the polished mahogany table Joey Hill, the show's producer, was readying a stack of notes. Tom wasn't sure what he thought of Joey yet, but he had to admit that Joey certainly looked like a hard-nosed producer. With his mop of unruly black hair accented by the three different pencils stuck behind his ears, Joey looked like something central casting would come up with for the role of a harried newsman.

"OK, crew, listen up," Joey said as he arranged some papers in front of him. He took a swig from his coffee cup and unwrapped a sandwich as he waited for everybody to get settled. "Kenny, the bright kid over in research, just heard an interesting tidbit over the grapevine." Joey waved his hands toward Kenny, who looked slightly embarrassed at being singled out.

"You mean the item in *The Hollywood Page* about all those young movie stars serving time in prison?" Ron piped up.

"Hmmm . . . stars behind bars . . ." Joey took a bite of his meatball hero, his expression intrigued. "Sounds good, but it will keep. Kenny's come up with something hot that we needed film on as of five minutes ago. We're talking a real scorcher, kids. Let's have it, Kenny."

"Uh . . ." Kenny cleared his throat as everyone looked at him expectantly. "I heard about this off-Broadway play that's being performed in the nude—"

"Starkers," Joey said with relish as he licked some tomato sauce off his hand.

"Apparently some of the actors are reasonably young . . . ," Kenny continued.

"Young?" Joey barked out. "Infants! Barely legal! What did I tell you?" He nodded vigorously. "This stuff's *molten lava!*" He finished his sandwich and wiped his mouth on his sleeve. "I want plenty of footage on this. Jenny, you find out history on the playwright and director. Ron, you write up some commentary—how sad it is that the theater's resorted to shock tactics, yadda yadda."

Joey rubbed his hands together in glee. "That's *our* take on the situation," he explained. "We exploit it as much as possible, but our position is how moral standards have fallen. That kind of garbage. You know the drill."

He paused proudly and looked around the table. "You." He pointed to Tom. "Whistle up a camera crew. Hop to it. What's the address, Kenny?"

Kenny looked down at his notes. "The Maxwell Theater."

The Maxwell! Tom's jaw dropped. *That's where*

Elizabeth is! This must *be the work of one of her weirdo colleagues.* Tom broke out in a cold sweat. *But . . . what's she going to say when I show up with a crew from* Tease-n-Tell?

"Hey, Tommy, I'm talking to you," Joey snapped.

"Sorry," Tom replied. He tried to concentrate on what Joey was saying, but visions of his imminent demise crowded his head.

"One word of advice, kid," Joey began. "Don't tell the people at the theater that you're from *Tease-n-Tell.* I don't know why, but some people don't like us." Joey looked genuinely confused. "Anyway, tell them something like . . . I don't know . . . like you're from—"

"A classy cable newsmagazine currently in development," Tom suggested wearily.

"That's it!" Joey snapped his fingers and peered at Tom closely. "I like you, kid. You're sharp. All right, everybody out of here. The next time we meet, I want to be looking at one sizzler of a program."

After the meeting broke up, Tom resisted the urge to bury his head in his hands and moan. *There's got to be some way out of this,* he thought miserably.

"Hey, Tom, hurry up," a camera operator called out as he rushed by.

"I'm coming." Tom pushed his chair back from the table. His movements had all the energy of a man on his way to his own funeral. *Maybe that's the answer,* Tom thought as he walked out of the conference room. *Maybe I should just throw myself in front of a cab. After all, it will only hurt for a second. The grief that I get from Elizabeth will last a* lot *longer!*

Let's see, if I change Gavin's line on page twenty-three, then maybe it would make sense. . . .
"Oh, what am I doing." Elizabeth threw her notebook down in frustration. She was sitting alone on the stage of the Maxwell, trying to come up with some solutions to the new set of problems that had been dumped in her lap. "There's absolutely no way that my play makes sense as a one-woman show. I must be losing my mind to even consider going along with Hildy and her lunatic ideas."

Elizabeth dangled her legs over the edge of the stage. Only the work lights were on, illuminating the small particles of dust floating through the air. The theater was totally silent, and the atmosphere was slightly spooky. *Well, I guess that's appropriate,* she mused. *After all, my play has turned into a horror show.*

Elizabeth stretched the kinks out of her back as she stood up and walked over to Gavin's desk. She ran her hands over the burled wood surface and picked up one of the papier-mâché statuettes that served as the prop journalism awards. "Young Journalists' Citation for Excellence," she read with a small smile on her face. The trophy was an exact copy of one that Tom had back on his desk at WSVU, the campus television station.

She frowned as the quiet was shattered by a burst of loud noise. "What's all that racket?" she murmured. "Did someone let a herd of elephants in here?" Elizabeth jerked her head over to the stage door entrance just in time to see Tom come bursting in, loaded down with equipment, a camera crew at his heels.

"Tom!" Elizabeth cried out, stunned. She scrambled off the stage and ran to greet him. "What are you doing here? You didn't come to take footage of the rehearsal, did you?"

"Yeah," one of the crew members said. "Where are all the nake—hey! Watch what you're doing!" he yelled as Tom stumbled backward, nearly toppling him to the floor.

"Sorry," Tom mumbled. "I, uh, lost my balance. This microphone is heavier than I thought."

Elizabeth glanced at the microphone doubtfully, then back at Tom. "You're here to get some footage?" she asked, unsure of exactly what was going on.

"Yeah." Tom nodded, zombielike. "We're here to get some footage."

"That's right," another crew member piped up. "We're supposed to get lots of hot film on the nud—"

"Tom! Are you all right?" Elizabeth gasped as

122

Tom bent double in a fit of coughing so violent that it was impossible to hear anything else within a fifty-yard radius.

"I'll—be—fine," Tom finally managed to gasp out.

Tom doesn't seem like himself, Elizabeth thought. *He's not usually so clumsy either. Since when has a microphone been too heavy for Tom to handle? Maybe he's just really nervous—first day on the job and all that.* Her face softened in sympathy as she drew closer to him.

"It's just *incredible* that you're here!" she whispered, touched beyond words. "You must have had to *beg* your story editor to get a crew over to the Maxwell. I mean, I'm sure that a start-up show has more important things to cover than some unknown college playwrights. I'm . . . I'm sure this story was *your* idea, right?"

Tom coughed again. *"Right,"* he choked out.

"This is so sweet, Tom," Elizabeth said, her eyes sparkling with delight. "It means a lot to know you'd do something like this . . . for me."

"Sure," Tom mumbled.

He seems to have an awful lot of trouble looking me in the eye, Elizabeth thought, puzzled, before recognition dawned on her. *Maybe he didn't tell anyone I was his girlfriend! Uh-oh—I can't have Tom accused of nepotism on his first day!*

"Thank you, *all* of you," Elizabeth said loudly to the rest of the crew. "This kind of press—it's a terrific break for us all. And *completely unexpected*," she directed toward Tom.

One of the techs stopped midway in putting down his soda can, his eyes wide. "You mean you're gonna take off your—"

"Tom!" Elizabeth cried, reaching out to catch him as he toppled over backward right into the arms of the tech.

"What's going on?" Claire demanded imperiously as she strode smack-dab into the middle of the melee. "My cast could hear you from our rehearsal room." Her combat boots tapped out a staccato rhythm against the floorboards. With her black turtleneck and army fatigue pants, she looked like a general addressing her troops. Except most generals, Elizabeth knew, didn't wear black lipstick and raccoon eyeliner.

"Claire, guess what?" Elizabeth turned toward Claire, her face lit by an enthusiastic smile. "This is my boy—uh, this is Tom Watts. Tom, I'd like you to meet Claire Sterling, one of my fellow playwrights and directors." Tom extended his hand, which Claire acknowledged with a nod.

"Tom's here to shoot some footage of rehearsals. He just got this great job," Elizabeth said proudly. "He's working for, um . . ."

"A classy cable newsmagazine currently in development," the tech crew chorused robotically.

Elizabeth spun back to look at the crew in astonishment. "Well, yes." She turned back to

Claire. "Tom's working for this really classy program, a new cable show, and he's here to get some footage on the current theater scene."

"Is that so?" Claire quirked an eyebrow. "In that case, you'll want to come and see *my* rehearsal. It's definitely the hottest thing going on."

"It would be kind of hard to get any footage of my play right now, Tom," Elizabeth said apologetically. "Hildy's on a lunch break, and even when she comes back, Ken's unavailable. You might have to get me another time."

Possibly never! she added silently, glowering. *Here Tom arranges this wonderful opportunity for me, and I have* nothing *to show for it!*

"Hey." One of the crew members tugged on her sleeve as he followed everyone out the door. "You're really quick, I mean about us being from a classy newsmagazine and all." He gave Elizabeth a wink.

Now what was that about? Elizabeth wondered. *Whatever. I'm sure Tom knows what he's doing, so for now . . . I'm just going to stay out of his way,* she resolved with a shake of her head as she returned to her notes.

Chapter
Nine

How do I get myself into these situations? Tom wondered miserably. He massaged his temples as he followed Claire, his camera crew in tow. His head felt like a drum being played from the inside, and sweat was trickling in rivulets down his back.

I just hope this Claire character decided to rehearse her cast with clothes on today, he prayed silently. *No nude actors, no nude footage. No nude footage, no Tease-n-Tell story. No Tease-n-Tell story, no problem with Elizabeth!*

"I think you'll find my play is a departure from the sentimental, bourgeois drivel that passes for theater these days," Claire lectured as she strode confidently down the hall. "You might recognize one or two of my actors. Vince Klee is—"

"Vince Klee is in your cast?" Tom sputtered in disbelief.

"Oh, don't worry," Claire hastened to add. "I

haven't given in to the demands of commercialism. Vince just had the right . . . *qualities* for the part."

Has Elizabeth been seeing Vince Klee naked every day? Tom wondered, his jaw dropping open and his stomach plummeting toward his knees at the thought.

"Well, here we are," Claire announced. She swung the door of the studio open dramatically. "Feast your eyes on the future of theater, gentlemen."

Tom could barely bring himself to look. He was too afraid of what he might find. Naked performers would mean that *Tease-n-Tell* would have a juicy broadcast. *And when Elizabeth realizes what show I'm really working for, I'll feel so ashamed!* Tom thought, resisting the urge to cover his eyes with his hands.

On the other hand, it doesn't really matter, he reasoned. *Because if I see Vince Klee naked, the sight'll make me too miserable to care about anything else!* Tom decided to stand in the entranceway, his eyes glued to the floor as if he found his shoelaces endlessly fascinating.

"Hey, Tom, what's your problem? Let us through!" The camera crew pushed him aside and barreled into the room.

Tom stayed where he was, his eyes at shoe level. *Not that any of these guys are wearing shoes,* he thought, his gaze flitting around the floor. *But*

128

so what? Bare feet doesn't necessarily mean bare everything else.

He mustered the courage to raise his eyes to knee level. *Naked knee level, that is . . . but maybe a lot of the actors are wearing shorts,* Tom thought hopefully.

He lifted his eyes higher. *Well, that guy is* definitely *naked. Yup,* she *certainly is too!* Tom looked away quickly, his face flaming in embarrassment. Without warning, his glance fell on Vince Klee—the *upper* half of Vince Klee, that is.

Well, so that's what Vince Klee's incredibly buff, well-built, muscled-to-the-max chest and biceps really look like, Tom noted miserably as he felt his own toned physique dwindling into toothpicks and marshmallows.

"Tom! Hey, what are you doing here?" Vince bounded over, his script rolled up under his arm.

"Hi, Vince." Tom kept his eyes riveted to Vince's own, afraid to look lower than his chin.

"So? What's going on? You're here to get some film on us?" Vince unfurled his script and tossed it playfully in the air. "Whoops!" he said as it fell to the ground.

"I'll get it," Tom said automatically. He bent to retrieve the script, which was lying midway between his own loafers and Vince's bare feet.

Tom paused in his bent position. He surreptitiously slid his eyes over to Vince's feet. *Well, the guy's not wearing shoes, and he's not wearing a shirt, so—does he have anything at all on in be-tween?* Tom brought his line of vision as high as Vince's ankles, which were sedately clad in denim. Tom was so happy at the sight, he almost started dancing.

"Here you go." He tossed the script back to Vince.

"So what's the name of the show you're working for?" Vince asked. "I know a lot of people in the industry. Some of my best friends work the technical side. Who knows, I may have hooked up with somebody from your group on another shoot."

Tom stared at him blankly. "Name?"

"Yeah." Vince raised a puzzled eyebrow. "You know, what the show is *called*."

"Hey, Tom," a crew member called. "Where should I set these lights?"

Phew! Tom sighed in relief. "Uh, listen, Vince, I'd better get busy. Later." Tom flung the words over his shoulder as he hurried to join his crew.

I'd better come up with some believable info on the show—and quick, Tom thought as he looked through the camera lens. "Looks good, guys." He nodded. "We might want to bounce some light off that wall to get rid of those shadows on that actress's . . . um, on that actress," Tom finished lamely. He bent his head to the camera lens again.

Looks OK . . . little worried about that backdrop . . . doesn't add to composition . . . how about—whoa! Tom almost whistled as Vince Klee appeared in the viewfinder. His great looks hadn't escaped Tom's notice before, but somehow the camera's lens made them even more dramatic.

Who cares that he's wearing jeans? Tom thought, fighting back a wave of insecurity. *That doesn't change the fact that he's a rich movie star who's seeing an awful lot of my girlfriend lately— correction—*she's *seeing an awful lot of* him!

Jessica's lungs felt as if they would burst and her legs screamed in agony as she attempted to scale the sheer surface of the Sheetrock. The sun blazed down mercilessly and sweat poured down Jessica's face, but she didn't dare wipe it off. Both her hands were gripping the rock for dear life as she struggled with the wall-climbing exercise that Pruitt had devised as a little afternoon treat.

Trust Pruitt to come up with something like this, Jessica thought grimly. *As if I really need to know how to scale a wall! Puh-leeze. When I'm guarding Vince Klee, I'll be much more likely to go windsurfing than wall scaling.*

Jessica grimaced as her hands scrabbled for an easier hold on the rock. Her palms were scratched and bleeding, and she wanted to grasp something less punishing than the pointed outcropping she now held. Jessica spotted a bump in the rock a few inches overhead. *That's more like it,* she thought, relinquishing her current grip with one hand and reaching out as far as she could.

Just a little bit more, Jessica urged as her fingers crept upward. Her arm lunged forward, but she'd miscalculated the distance. Her legs kicked the air wildly as she lost her footing. *I won't fall,* she told herself. *I won't!* Jessica stopped kicking and focused all her energy on hanging on. Out of the corner of her eye she could see Harlan having his own troubles, and behind her, about three feet down, she could hear another recruit panting for breath.

Jessica twisted her head as far as possible so that she could see the ground, where the rest of the recruits were waiting their turn to make their assault on the rock face. *It looks so far away!* she thought, her stomach contracting in fear. Her gaze connected with Pruitt's; even though they were separated by a large distance, Jessica could feel menace radiating from her.

What's her problem? Jessica wondered. *I'm going to be dead after the fight tomorrow! What more does she want?*

Jessica took a deep breath and concentrated. *Wait a second,* she told herself. *What if I make it to the top first? That would show Pruitt I'm not so easy to break!*

The thought gave Jessica stamina, and she managed to get a foothold higher up. *All right!* she cheered silently. *Let's see who's got a sorry sorority girl butt now!*

With her legs secure, Jessica had the confidence

to swing farther out. She quickly moved higher, barely wincing as the hard rock sent agonizing pain shooting through her.

I don't care how much it hurts, she resolved. *I don't care if it's the last thing I do! I'm going to show Pruitt just what Jessica Wakefield is made of!*

With a final burst of energy Jessica reached the top and pulled herself over. "Yes!" Jessica raised a fist in victory. She looked down at Harlan and beyond him to the recruits still waiting.

Where are Sunshine, Annette, and Bev? Jessica shielded her eyes with her hand and scanned the ground until she found them. She waved and jumped up and down to get their attention, but they were oblivious to her antics.

Why aren't they cheering for me? she thought peevishly. *They should be totally psyched!* But they were so busy whispering among themselves, they didn't even appear to notice her triumph.

What's going on? Jessica frowned in irritation. Her irritation turned to fear as a sudden doubt flickered through her mind. *First they hatched a strange plot they wouldn't even let me in on,* she realized, *and now they're not even acting like they're on my side!* Her stomach plummeted to the ground below. *What if they're turning against me? Or worse!* Jessica gasped. *What if they've always been against me?*

"So, Elizabeth, do we agree?" Hildy paused and looked at Elizabeth expectantly but didn't wait for a response. "It makes *sense* to see the play as a struggle between the split personalities of a schizophrenic, doesn't it? I feel that the differences between Gavin and Phoebe will be so much more *heartfelt* if they're really one and the same person."

It's a good thing that Tom and his crew didn't get any footage of this! Elizabeth thought morosely as Hildy shucked off her vest and tie and donned what looked like a suit of armor.

"I was lucky the costume designer had something like this," Hildy crowed as she buckled the sides of a metal-plated vest. "I feel it's a perfect symbol of Gavin's overbearing masculinity *and* an expression of the hidden combative nature that lurks inside Phoebe."

"Uh-huh," Elizabeth murmured, unable to dignify Hildy's ramblings with a reasonable answer.

Hildy had restructured the play so much that it was hard to tell what scene they were on. *Isn't this the part where Phoebe's supposed to say she'd never reveal a source?* Elizabeth wondered as she listened in vain for the words she'd written, but they seemed to have been replaced by a monologue about how the media's images of women were unrealistic.

So OK, I didn't exactly write Hamlet, *but I sure didn't write anything this bad either!* Elizabeth sighed. She closed her eyes, too dispirited to continue watching, and thought back to when she had started writing the play for her modern dramatic theory seminar. She had been both thrilled

134

and trepidant about trying her hand at a new form of writing. *It didn't go that well in the beginning either,* Elizabeth recalled. She'd been inspired by an argument she'd had with Tom, and once she'd gotten started, it had been hard for her to stop. But she'd had more than a few troubles trying to work through her dialogue.

How did I get over that? Elizabeth wondered. She crinkled her brow, trying to remember. *Of course! Jessica!* Visions of Jessica sitting on her bed in the room they shared in Dickenson Hall sprang to her eyes. Jessica had acted out entire scenes from the play while Elizabeth had watched, fascinated. *It made such a difference to have Jess breathe life into the words,* she recalled. *I could tell what worked and what didn't. But then again, she's ten times the actress Hildy is!*

Elizabeth blocked out the screeching sound of Hildy's voice so that Jessica's voice could come floating back to her.

"Don't you see, Elizabeth?" Jessica had pranced around the room, her purple satin comforter wrapped around her like a ball gown. *"The awards ceremony is the perfect place for Phoebe and Gavin to reconcile. That's when he truly respects her as a reporter, and besides, she gets to look awesome!"* And Elizabeth, who knew more about overalls and baseball caps than ball gowns, was able to come up with the most moving and romantic scene in the play with her sister's help.

135

It's too bad that Jessica isn't here now, Elizabeth thought sadly. *Not only would I have a lot more fun, but the audience would too!*

Elizabeth stirred restlessly in her seat; her memories made her miss her sister terribly. If she closed her eyes, she could see Jessica tripping around in her satin comforter, looking strangely elegant. But the images of Jessica in a makeshift purple satin ball gown were suddenly wiped out and replaced with a vision of Jessica swathed in bandages. *The boxing match!* Elizabeth's eyes flew open. *I've got to talk to Jessica!*

"Hildy! Let's take a break!" Elizabeth called out, cutting Hildy off in midsentence.

The actress looked at her in surprise. "But I just got back from lunch," she whined. "Besides, I really feel like I'm on the verge of a breakthrough right now. I don't want to interrupt the flow!"

"I can see you're on the edge of something big," Elizabeth said, biting the inside of her cheek in order to keep a straight face. "That's why I think we should take a break. You're going to need to, um, realign your energies to be able to channel the force of your ideas."

She smiled in satisfaction as Hildy's mouth dropped open in astonishment. "Elizabeth! I had *no idea* you were so sensitive to my aura! You're absolutely *right!* I *could* use a meditation break. You see? Now that Ken's out of the way, we're really developing a rapport!"

As soon as Hildy lay down on the stage to meditate, Elizabeth grabbed her wallet and ran to the pay phone. She took out her phone card and, holding her breath, began to dial.

"You're wanted in the office, Wakefield. Fall out."

Jessica's stomach clenched in fear at the abrupt summons. She saluted the officer and fell out of the single-file march.

What now? she wondered tiredly. *I'm so wiped, I don't have the strength to deal with* anything.

But as Jessica hurried to the office she couldn't help feeling that something was up. *Maybe Commander Phipps wants to see me,* she guessed anxiously. *Maybe Pruitt got me in trouble!*

Jessica entered the office, fully expecting to be faced with a firing squad. Instead she was confronted by two secretaries discussing hair-conditioning treatments.

Puh-leeze, Jessica thought with a smirk. *Don't they know that hot oil treatments are totally passé?* She cleared her throat. "Uh, excuse me. I was told to report."

"Report what?" one of the secretaries asked. She snapped her gum and scrutinized Jessica head to toe.

"Uh, report *here,*" Jessica replied, feeling more nervous by the second.

"Oh yeah. Is your name Wakefield?"

Jessica nodded dumbly. *She's going to tell me*

that I've been singled out for some gruesome punishment, she mused. *She'll say that—*

"You got a phone call. You can go in there"— she gestured to an empty room—"if you want some privacy."

A phone call? Is that all? Jessica nearly swooned in relief as she skipped into the empty room and grabbed the phone excitedly.

"Jess, is that you?" Elizabeth's voice floated over the wire.

"Elizabeth!" Jessica squealed in delight.

"Jessica, I wanted to know what was going on with the boxing match."

"Oh, *that.*" Jessica's voice was flat. She twisted the phone cord nervously. "It's still on."

"Jessica! You're going to get yourself killed!" Elizabeth shrieked.

"Look, Elizabeth. Things aren't as bad as I thought." She lowered her voice dramatically. "I have a plan."

"Oh, great." Elizabeth didn't sound as relieved as Jessica had expected her to.

Elizabeth knows *how good I am at planning and plotting,* Jessica thought. *So why doesn't she sound more excited?* She twirled her hair around her fingers and frowned as she noticed a split end. *Maybe hot oil* isn't *passé. . . .*

"Jess," Elizabeth said in her best I'm-four-minutes-older voice, "you know how your plans usually turn out—*backfiring!*"

"That is just not true!" Jessica replied, stung. She stared at the receiver in indignation, as if Elizabeth could see her.

"OK. Name *one* time your plans worked out."

"I could name a hundred," Jessica replied confidently. "There was that time I pretended to be you and . . . well, OK, there was that time when I took the money out of your bank—all right, *look,* what about the time I . . . aw, come on, Liz," Jessica cried in exasperation. "Just because you don't believe in me—and *no one else* does either—doesn't mean I can't take care of myself!" Jessica swallowed the lump in her throat. "I can take care of myself just *fine,* thank you. I don't need *anybody's* help!"

Good thing, Jessica thought, *'cause it looks like I'm not going to be getting any either!* Jessica slammed the phone down angrily, squared her shoulders, and stood up straight. *This is it. I'm on my own. It's Jessica Wakefield against the world. And I'm going to come out on top—no matter what it takes!*

Chapter Ten

"I *really* need a break," Elizabeth said with a groan. She stifled a yawn and looked longingly at the leather armchairs that lined the perimeter of the room. The lobby was as Old World and elegant as the rest of the theater. Photos from noteworthy productions adorned the walls, the wallpaper was the same deep red as the theater seats, and the club chairs looked cozy and inviting.

Very cozy and very inviting, Elizabeth amended. With a heartfelt sigh she flopped down in one of the armchairs and closed her eyes. *Why do I feel so strung out?* she wondered. *Let's see, could it have anything to do with the fact that my lead actor just walked and my sister is about to be dismembered?*

Elizabeth sighed. *Maybe I should have been more supportive about Jessica's plan,* she thought, her brow furrowing. *I didn't want to hurt her, but her plans* do *have a way of backfiring. . . .*

"Elizabeth?"

Her eyes flew open at the sound of her name, whispered softly in her ear.

"Vince—I thought I was alone." Elizabeth blushed slightly as she looked deep into Vince's incredible dark eyes. He was kneeling down by the chair, and his face was level with hers.

"I hope you don't mind that I decided to join you." He returned her smile, his eyes crinkling at the corners. "But I wanted to find out how your rehearsal went now that Ken's gone."

"Well, let's just put it this way. I now truly understand the meaning of the word *apocalypse*."

"That bad, huh?" Vince looked sympathetic as he sat himself on the arm of her chair. "To tell you the truth, my rehearsal didn't go much better."

"I'm sorry. . . . I guess we're both caught in no-win situations." She sighed deeply.

"C'mon, Elizabeth, what's really going on with you?" Vince asked, his voice filled with concern. "I mean besides the obvious, you seem really down. Anything I can help with?" Vince inquired gently.

"You're too sweet, Vince." Elizabeth touched his hand. "But I don't want to talk about it right now."

"I'm here for you if you need me," Vince said quietly, his eyes boring deeply into hers as he returned the pressure of her hand. "Look—if you don't want to talk about your problems, how about

I burden you with mine? I'm stuck in a play that makes *Attack of the Killer Tomatoes* seem like *Romeo and Juliet,* the director is a lunatic, the other actors don't seem to care, and the costumes . . ." He rolled his eyes. "I guess I can't truthfully say the costumes are bad."

"How can you pass judgment on something that doesn't even exist?" Elizabeth asked lightly, hoping Vince couldn't see her blush.

He chuckled ruefully. "In fact, I'd have to say that the whole experience is disturbing my *aura!*" He gave the words a pretentious accent.

Elizabeth's eyes opened wide, and she burst into laughter. "Vince, you've—you've *channeled* Hildy!"

"Really?" Vince drawled. "You feel I was able to accurately radiate negative energy? Of course," he continued, smoothing back his black curly hair, "I *do* applaud the fact that she doesn't bother with middle-class notions of *cleanliness.* Her *aura* may be contaminated, but not by *deodorant!*"

Elizabeth snickered behind her hand. "That's a *perfect* Gerald!" she whispered. "I swear—you were *completely* obnoxious just now. In fact, you're kind of *scaring* me."

"Don't be frightened, Liz. I'm just a child of the revolution." Vince's dark eyes sparkled mischievously. "You're allowing your bourgeois upbringing to taint your conception of my true self, i.e., that which is, like, *me.*"

"Actually it makes sense that you'd be able to assume the *negative* traits of Gerald's personality," Elizabeth trilled nasally. "After all, you both share the bond of the *patriarchy*."

Vince raised his eyebrows. "But Hildy," Vince snapped, capturing Claire's strident tones to perfection. "Performing nude is the *only* way of dealing with the patriarchal issue. After all, when you objectify the body to such an extent, it has the opposite effect, rendering it . . . completely unobjectified!" Vince wiped his forehead. "Phew! You know what, Elizabeth?" He snickered. "I don't think I even understand what I just said!"

"Well, Claire never makes any sense either."

Vince threw back his head and laughed. "I thought I was the only one that didn't understand her!"

"Oh, please, Vince, you're so *naive*. Sometimes I forget you're from Hollywood!"

Elizabeth's laughter rang out to meet Vince's; she felt as if her sides would split as she leaned against his shoulder, her tears of happiness falling on his black shirt as if they belonged there.

Jessica peeked out of the broom closet and surveyed the corridor. *Pruitt* would *come marching down the hall when the only place to hide is a closet full of icky cleaning stuff,* Jessica thought as she untangled a mop from her hair. *But this time the joke's on her! Now I know that she's safely out of the way, I can case her office.*

She stepped out of the closet, ignoring the crash of brooms and buckets as she closed the door, and glanced furtively up and down the hall. Seeing that she was unobserved, she crept stealthily toward Pruitt's office.

Although Jessica had a legitimate appointment to clean the office during dinner, she couldn't bring herself to wait that long. *How can I hang around the barracks studying surveillance techniques when there's a simply delicious mystery waiting to be solved?* she asked herself, her eyes sparkling in anticipation of the secrets to be uncovered.

She entered the office, closed the door carefully behind her, and sashayed over to the desk, where several data printout sheets were displayed for her viewing pleasure. *Mmm, what's this?* she wondered, intrigued.

Jessica's brow furrowed as she studied the pages. On one of them Harlan's name was circled in red. *What does that mean?* she wondered. *Does the evil drillmaster have a crush on Harlan the Horrible?* Jessica giggled as she leafed through the rest of the pages, pausing when her attention was caught by some more red markings. "Wait . . . she's circled two other guys too," she murmured. "I don't get it. Do they have some connection with Harlan? Maybe they're next on her date-mate list. . . ." Smirking, Jessica racked her memory for a memory of the other two victims.

"Got it!" Jessica snapped her fingers. "They're all aces on the rifle range!" Jessica dropped the data sheets and rubbed her arms. *Something freaky's going on,* she noted with a shiver. *Why would Pruitt be keeping tabs on the three best shots at FSSA?*

Jessica sat down in Pruitt's desk chair and rested her chin on her hand. *Is there some way that I can use that information?* she thought, puzzled. *Well, maybe it doesn't matter. Let's see what the key holds in store!*

Eyes gleaming with excitement, Jessica rooted through the drawer. She peeled the key away from where it was taped and tossed it up in the air triumphantly.

"Now just what exactly does *this* little jewel open?" she murmured, staring at the key as if it were a five-carat diamond. She squinted to make out the tiny lettering that adorned its side. *Goldline? Now what does that mean?* Jessica tried the key in one of the locked desk drawers. No dice. She shook her head, her heart plummeting.

Jessica looked around the office with a sigh and swallowed her disappointment. Then her eye fell on the battered filing cabinet. Goldline Office Systems was stamped in faded copper on its side.

"Yeah, baby!" Jessica cheered softly. She jumped to her feet and ran over to the file cabinet, her heart beating as if it would burst.

Jessica slid out the drawer and stared at the

146

treasure trove in front of her. Humming a little tune, she reached for the files inside with a happy smile on her face. *Harlan P. Edwards—DOB—who cares? Social security—so what? Prison record . . .*

"*Excuse* me?" Jessica screeched. "Assault? B and E? That's *quite* a record." Jessica whistled, impressed by how much of a scumbag Harlan was turning out to be. "I guess those tales of playing bodyguard to India Jordan were dreamed up in the joint!" she hissed, remembering the stack of lies he'd fed to her during the plane trip on the way to Florida.

"Who else is in here?" she muttered, flipping through the stack of files. "Sunshine? *Car theft?* No way!" Jessica rocked back on her heels, stunned. *I guess I shouldn't be surprised,* she noted, her heart sinking. *She hot-wired that truck like a pro!* Jessica sighed, recalling how they'd been stuck on an obstacle course on Monday with a dead vehicle until Sunshine put her special "skills" to use. Quickly flipping through the rest of the files, Jessica found Annette's. Her record showed that she'd been rejected from the Tucson Police Academy due to shoplifting violations as a teenager. As for Bev, she'd once been convicted . . . of armed robbery.

"Armed robbery? At *fifteen?*" Jessica shook her head, tears filling her eyes. "This is unbelievable. I thought they were my friends! With records like these, they must be against—"

Jessica gasped and stood stock-still. *Footsteps,*

she realized. *Leaden, herd-of-buffalo footsteps!*

Moving quickly, Jessica shoved the files back in the cabinet and relocked it. *The key!* Jessica scrambled back to the desk and fumbled with the piece of tape. She had just secured it to its sticking place when Pruitt appeared in the doorway.

Curses, Jessica thought, her heart sinking. *Caught red-handed!* She met Pruitt's venomous gaze as she slowly withdrew her hand from the desk. "I was looking for some . . . air freshener," she finished lamely. "The air in here is so stuffy. . . ."

"Save it!" Pruitt barked. "It's people like you that give the security industry a bad name, Wakefield." She threw the door wide open. "Now get out."

Jessica stalked past her. While Jessica wasn't happy about being caught, Pruitt didn't really rattle her. Jessica had listened to her bad-girl act enough times to know she wasn't as tough as she was pretending to be.

"I'll tell you one thing, princess." Pruitt jutted her lantern jaw at Jessica. "I'm going to make good and sure that the closest you get to the security industry is cleaning up after guard dogs. After Saturday you won't even be able to walk, let alone finish your training." Pruitt dusted her knuckles against her chin and grinned sadistically.

OK. Now *I'm rattled!* Jessica thought with a wince as she slunk away, feeling like the loneliest, most doomed person on earth.

*   *   *

148

"You know, Vince is right about Hildy," Elizabeth said thoughtfully.

"Hmm? What about?" Tom asked. *Who cares what about?* he added silently. *Doesn't Elizabeth know that I just want to hold her in my arms right now—not talk about her play?*

Tom sighed as he looked at Elizabeth all curled up on the couch next to him, looking sexy and innocent at the same time.

"I bet she really *did* escape from the circus!" Elizabeth giggled.

"I bet she did," Tom said absently. He leaned forward and kissed Elizabeth's cheek softly. *C'mon, Liz,* Tom silently urged. *Those little butterfly kisses usually drive you wild—what's going on here?*

It seemed to Tom that the amount of time he and Elizabeth spent locked in each other's embrace had dwindled dangerously in the past few days. *I know we're not going to be making love,* Tom thought with a twinge. *But does that mean we can't make time for making out?*

"Vince thinks I let Hildy get under my skin too much," Elizabeth continued.

Tom leaned back with a sigh.

"He may be right," she continued with a faraway smile. "I mean, Vince has a lot more experience with these things than I have, so he's really clear on how to handle them. Things would be a lot harder without Vince around."

I don't believe it! Tom fumed. *How many times did she manage to say Vince's name in the past thirty seconds?*

Tom felt his spine stiffen at the realization, and he held his own mug of chamomile tea so tightly that he feared he might shatter it. *I should be having a good time,* he thought bitterly. *Here I am, after a hard day at work, having a nice cup of tea with a beautiful woman that I happen to be in love with. So what's the problem?*

"I wish Vince was around to help me out more often." Elizabeth interrupted Tom's train of thought. "Of course, he's *so* busy with his own rehearsals. . . ."

Duh, Vince is the problem, Tom answered himself. *No . . . Elizabeth's* fascination *with him is.* He rolled his eyes in irritation. *What does she see in him anyway? The guy's in a* nudie *play!* Tom scowled as he recalled seeing Vince's sculpted upper body at the *Tease-n-Tell* shoot. Somehow Vince's jealousy-inspiring muscles seemed to be the only thing he could remember from his first day on the job.

"I really respect how he came to New York to get some grounding in the theater—"

Tom snorted loudly.

"Is something wrong?" Elizabeth asked.

"Nothing," Tom mumbled, burying his face in his mug. *Grounding in the theater?* he asked himself, outraged. *Since when did nudie cutie shows get to be considered serious theater? It would serve him right if* Tease-n-Tell *trashed him!*

Tom snickered to himself as he imagined the kind of profile that *Tease-n-Tell* could do on Vince Klee. *They'll make a laughingstock of him!* he thought with glee. *They'll* ground *him in the theater, all right! They'll make* mincemeat *of him! They'll . . . wait a second.* Tom sat up sharply, an unpleasant thought pricking at his conscience. *What am I* thinking? *If* Tease-n-Tell *goes ahead with the piece, they'll tar Elizabeth with the same brush! They'll ruin her!*

Already Tom could see Elizabeth's angelic face streaked with tears of sorrow—for Vince. Tom closed his eyes as he imagined Elizabeth comforting Vince—and Vince's arms snaking their way around her. *And as if that isn't bad enough, she'll figure out* I'm *the one who filmed the whole thing!* he realized, his deceit crashing down hard on him. *She'll scream at me, murder me—even break up with me!*

"Are you all right, Tom?" Elizabeth asked, her sweet face creased with concern. "You seem awfully distracted. Was the first day on the new job really hard?"

"Uh, well, I . . . ," Tom stammered, overcome by feelings of guilt. "I guess I'm just a little tired," he explained lamely. "Maybe a little TV will help me relax."

Elizabeth nodded as Tom picked up the remote and clicked on the TV. "I'm sorry—I probably wore you out with my chattering," she said with an easy smile. She glanced at the TV briefly and began idly leafing through one of Tish's aromatherapy books.

Tom channel-surfed aimlessly for a few seconds, but his mind was still tied up in knots. If only he could come up with a way— *"Monday: Is this a theater or a high-class peep show?"* the TV blared suddenly. Startled, Tom jumped and nearly dropped the remote as the screen came to life with a commercial for the next episode of *Tease-n-Tell.*

"What's that about?" Elizabeth looked up just as Tom, fumbling with the remote, managed to shut the set off.

"Huh?" Tom feigned confusion. "Oh . . . just trash." *Yeah, and I'm the one who filmed it,* he added silently. *I guess I don't have to worry about what'll happen when Elizabeth finds out the truth— this stress will kill me first.*

Jessica brushed out her long golden hair and scrutinized herself in the bathroom mirror. She peered at herself closely, trying to assess the damage done by her rigorous week at FSSA, just before lights-out on what could possibly turn out to be her last night in one piece.

Great—not only is my skin peeling, but my brows look horrendous! Jessica noted, drawing back in horror. Her arches were losing their distinctive shape, and there were more than a few stray hairs begging to be plucked. *But hey, I have to admit my body looks good.* She flexed her biceps right there in the women's barracks bathroom. *I look like I could whup butt! But will I?*

Jessica sobered at the question. She knew that tomorrow her reflection might very well be missing a few teeth—or worse. *Hopefully my mortician will have a solid beauty school background,* she thought, only half joking. *I must leave behind an exquisite corpse; otherwise my Theta sisters will never forgive me!*

Jessica moaned and dropped her brush. The notion of getting slaughtered, she had to admit, was a bit extreme. But the idea that her face was about to be rearranged was, sadly, *not.* She rummaged through her beauty bag for an eyebrow pencil and quickly began coloring in her two front teeth. *So that's how I'll look tomorrow night,* Jessica lamented, flashing a snaggletoothed smile at her reflection and choking back a sob.

"Something wrong?" Bev asked. She was standing at an adjacent sink, wearing fuzzy pajamas and brushing her teeth. Annette, in a black shortie nightgown, was borrowing Bev's toothpaste and wearing an equally quizzical expression.

"Oh, no worse than the usual," Jessica said sarcastically as she scrubbed away the eyebrow pencil. "I was just thinking that my beauty routine will be a lot easier tomorrow night. After all, I won't have to brush my teeth anymore after they've been knocked out."

"Forget about it, Jessica." Sunshine stepped out of one of the showers and wrapped herself in a towel. "Believe me, you *don't* need to worry about your smile."

Somehow that doesn't sound so reassuring, Jessica thought. *But maybe I'm just spooked because of what I found out about Sunshine today. I'm sure they're all trying to help me . . . right?*

"That's right," Annette echoed Sunshine. "*Everything's* taken care of." She gave Sunshine and Bev a decisive nod, and Bev winked back.

What's going on? Jessica wondered. *One minute they seem like they're on my side, the next . . . watch out! Am I just being paranoid, or am I being smart?*

Jessica studied the faces of her friends as they prepared for bed. Annette had finished with her teeth and was smoothing on some moisturizer. Bev was washing her face, and Sunshine was combing out her fiery hair. But they all had one thing in common: Underneath their placid expressions, something menacing lurked in their eyes.

I'm not *being paranoid!* Jessica assured herself with a frown. *I'm not! They* definitely *have it in for somebody—the question is, do they have it in for Pruitt . . . or* me?

Chapter
Eleven

"Excuse me," Tom said as he bumped into a young woman pushing a stroller. "Pardon me," he gasped breathlessly as he ran past an older man carrying groceries. "Sorry," he panted as he collided with a little boy dribbling a basketball.

How come everyone isn't home in bed on Saturday morning? Tom asked himself in irritation as he raced along the busy Midtown streets. Tom certainly wished that *he* were home in bed instead of weaving in and out of traffic.

But Tom had a mission. He had to get to *Tease-n-Tell* in time to try and stop the show. Tom knew that the theater exposé would be undergoing last minute editing in order to be ready for Monday's broadcast. *It's not too late!* he told himself as he narrowly missed being plowed down by a cab. *Joey will be there overseeing the editing. I just have to convince him to run another piece before he hands the tape over to the station!*

Tom ran flat out the final two blocks. He did a fifty-yard dash across the lobby, nearly fell flat on his face about ten separate times as he skidded on the polished marble floor, burst through the glass doors, and flew wheezing into the editing room.

"Hey, Tommy, slow down—life's too short," Joey said cheerfully. "Have you *seen* this footage? You're aces, kid!" He waved his hands excitedly toward where the footage Tom had shot was running in super–slow motion on five different monitors. "Not that you didn't have great subject matter, but still . . ."

Tom looked at the monitors, his heart sinking as he saw just how great the subject matter was. There was no denying that he'd been able to capture some extremely lurid images on the tape. Even if the actors weren't naked, the fact that they were speaking in tongues while doing a Balinese fertility dance would still make for an interesting *Tease-n-Tell* segment. *No wonder Joey thinks I did such a great job,* Tom realized with a gulp. *This stuff will make the* Tease-n-Tell *ratings go through the roof! How am I going to convince him not to show it?*

"What do you think? This stuff really smokes, huh?" Joey rubbed his hands together gleefully. "I'm going to go for a music video look, really sharp cuts but keep the edges soft, blur the figures." He took a sip of his coffee and winked at

Tom. "That way it will look even *juicier*, know what I mean?"

Tom nodded silently. *I know* exactly *what he means,* he thought grimly. *If he softens things up that way, even the people with clothes on will look naked!*

"You can't run this, Joey," he blurted out. "Please—you have to hand the network another reel."

"Can this piece? You crazy?" Joey swiveled in his chair to stare at Tom. "Say, are you one of those kids with a real uptight background?"

"No, no, nothing like that," Tom said hastily. "It's just that my girlfriend is involved with the show and—"

"Your girlfriend." Joey quirked an eyebrow and turned back to leer at the screen. "Your girlfriend's one of these?" He jerked his thumb at the monitor. "Jeez, some guys get all the luck." He shook his head in wonder.

He thinks Elizabeth is one of the nudie cuties! Tom realized, incensed. "My girlfriend *isn't* one of the cast," he explained.

"Oh." Joey's face fell. "Too bad, kid. Can't win them all."

"You don't understand," Tom persisted. "If you run this piece, Elizabeth will be miserable." *That's after she kills me,* Tom added silently.

"Let me get this straight," Joey said slowly. "You're telling your boss, the head producer, that

157

you want him to cancel a megahot segment?"

Tom nodded.

"And you want me to do this so you can keep your girlfriend happy?"

"Yes," Tom said eagerly. "You see, if—"

"Kid." Joey held up his hand to stop the flood of Tom's words. "Do I look stupid to you?"

"No, of course not. You're a really smart producer, Joey," Tom said honestly.

"Damn right I am." Joey paused. "Look, kid, I hate to screw up your relationship, but business is business, and really smart producers *don't* pull really hot shows."

"But—"

"No buts. You've got to learn to roll with the punches if you want to make it in TV."

Tom nodded miserably. He knew Joey was right. *After all, I've run dozens of shows at WSVU that I knew were going to upset plenty of people,* he reminded himself. *But somehow it never bothered me before.*

"Listen, I've got to go and see how one of the sound editors is getting on." Joey stood up and stretched. "Why don't you finish up the editing? Follow my notes—it's all down there." He handed Tom a clipboard covered with incomprehensible scrawls. "Once you see how good your work is, you'll feel differently. You'll be happy to have it air." Joey patted Tom on the shoulder as he left the screening room.

Yeah, right! Tom laughed sarcastically. *I'll be really happy when Elizabeth breaks up with me! And guess who will be waiting with his arms wide open to comfort her? The star of our show, Vince "Shirtless" Klee!*

With a sigh of resignation Tom moved over to the editing chair to cut his masterpiece.

Jessica walked down the long corridor, her gaze riveted on the closed double doors of the gym. She held her head high and ignored the gawking of the other recruits. *What was* that? Jessica wondered, startled by a loud noise. *Oh, that's just the beating of my heart. No biggie!*

A white terry cloth robe with her name emblazoned in red Magic Marker was draped across her shoulders. Sunshine, Annette, and Bev had given her the robe as a good luck charm. Jessica still wasn't sure if she could trust them or not, but she appreciated the gift and wore it as regally as if it were made of satin.

The spectators were silent. The only sound up and down the long corridor was the whisper of Jessica's robe as it trailed behind her. Her trio of maybe-friends brought up the rear of the procession in single file.

Jessica set the pace, walking in a slow and stately manner. Her posture was ramrod straight. The only indication of her nervousness was the slight tremor of her hands—otherwise Jessica

159

looked as confident as if she were walking to her own coronation. *I'd better look good,* she thought grimly. *Because I sure don't feel it.*

The doors of the gym loomed larger and larger, but time seemed to stand still. The seconds were as heavy as hours as the blood pounded furiously in Jessica's ears.

This is it, the last mile! Jessica thought with a gulp as her footsteps ate up the remaining distance that lay between her and the entrance to the gym. *This is how a paratrooper must feel before jumping out of a plane,* she realized, a chill playing along her backbone. *This is how a model must feel before she walks down a Paris catwalk—on a bad hair day!* Jessica shivered in disgust.

The procession approached the gym. Behind the closed doors Jessica could hear the screaming and cheering of the crowd. Jessica's knees nearly buckled underneath her. *This is it!* She gasped, stopping in front of the gym doors. She pictured the scene on the other side: hundreds of recruits, whipped up in a frenzy of excitement. She knew that some of them, perhaps *most* of them, were aching to see blood.

How many people will cheer when I fail? she asked herself, feeling more alone than she ever had in her entire eighteen years on the planet.

Jessica paused, her hand on the door and her heart in her throat. She closed her eyes briefly and uttered a silent prayer. *Good-bye, Elizabeth—find someone good to do my makeup for the funeral. Forgive me, Mom and Dad—don't let some weirdo boarder move into my room.* Sayonara, *Vince Klee—I did this all for you.*

She opened her eyes, inhaled deeply, and turned the door handle, prepared to meet her fate.

C'mon, Jess, pick up the phone, Elizabeth prayed as she tapped her foot. She'd been on hold for more than five minutes, waiting for a recruit to fetch Jessica, and she was beyond impatient.

Elizabeth nibbled absently on a croissant and looked out of Tish's kitchen window at the boats sailing on the Hudson. Normally the postcard-perfect view would have brought a smile to her face, but right now she was too keyed up to appreciate it. *Where is Jess already?* she wondered, fear gripping her in an icy, inescapable bear hug. *I've got to talk to her one last time before the fight. Maybe it's not too late to talk her out of it!*

"Hello?" She gripped the receiver as she heard someone pick up the phone on the other end. "Jessica?"

"Jessica Wakefield? Oh, she's not available right now. I'll have her call you back . . . that is, if she still *can* after her little get-together." The recruit snickered unpleasantly. "I've got to go. I wouldn't miss this match for the world."

Elizabeth hung up the phone slowly, her heart in her throat. *What if Jessica is already seriously injured?* Elizabeth wondered, her eyes brimming with tears. *What if she—*

The phone rang, jarring Elizabeth out of her unpleasant reverie. "Jess?" Elizabeth screamed after she picked up, holding the receiver so tightly, her knuckles turned white.

"Elizabeth? Is that you? It's Vince."

Elizabeth swallowed her disappointment. "Hi, Vince. What's up?" Elizabeth tried to sound bright and cheery for his sake, but she knew she sounded as scared as she felt.

"You tell me what's up," Vince replied, his voice hard and flat.

"Excuse me?" Elizabeth asked. She stared at the phone in confusion. "Is something wrong? You sound so—"

"Why don't you check out channel nine?" Vince let out a tight, sarcastic laugh. "You'll see what's going on, all right."

Bewildered, Elizabeth moved over to the kitchen work island where Tish kept a small portable TV and flicked it on. Gasping, she stared in disbelief at the picture on the screen. A shot of Vince filled the frame. It was clear that he wasn't wearing a shirt, but it wasn't clear if he had anything else on either.

"*Tease-n-Tell* tells it like it is," a voice announced, sounding particularly oily and slick. "And what a tease it is this time! Join us on Monday as Vince Klee, one of the hottest, hippest actors around, takes off his clothes and turns up the heat on his success thermostat. See him like you've never seen him before. Yes, folks—Vince Klee will steam up your screen as we show *revealing* rehearsal footage from—"

Elizabeth turned off the set, too sick to continue watching. She held on to the counter for support, afraid that if she didn't, she might topple over.

"How could you sell me out this way?" Vince demanded. "I thought we were friends, Elizabeth. I thought I could trust you. In fact, I thought that we were . . ." He trailed off.

"Vince," Elizabeth protested in shock as she moved over to one of the high stools and sat down. "How could you possibly think I had anything to do with this? I can't imagine who—"

The realization hit her like a bucket of ice water. *Tom!* Elizabeth gasped in shock. *This is all because of Tom! It has to be! And I thought his show was interested in unknown playwrights. . . . I thought he'd done this for me!* Elizabeth snorted in disgust—at Tom for stooping so low, at herself for being such a blind fool. *Classy cable newsmagazine, my foot. No wonder Vince is mad at me—he probably thinks I tipped Tom off!* Elizabeth stood up and began pacing back and forth; she was too unsettled to sit still.

"Vince, you've got to believe me, I had no idea what Tom was up to. If I had, I wouldn't have let him within a hundred yards of the Maxwell. I'm just as upset as you are." *That's putting it mildly!* Elizabeth fumed. *After I get through with Tom, he won't have the strength to stand up, let alone direct a camera crew!*

"You really expect me to believe that you didn't know what your boyfriend was up to?" Vince asked incredulously.

"Don't you understand, Vince? Tom *lied* to me!" Elizabeth choked out, her rage threatening to overwhelm her.

"He may have lied to you," Vince said quietly. "But it's *my* career he's trying to ruin."

"Oh, Vince," Elizabeth said helplessly. "I'm sorry. I don't know which is worse—the fact that Tom betrayed my trust or the fact that you're hurting." A vision of Vince distraught and Tom gloating flashed in front of Elizabeth's eyes.

Tom wouldn't gloat, she told herself. *He wouldn't have done this just to hurt me and Vince— or would he?* The thought was like a slap in the face. "Vince, I feel awful," she whispered.

"You sound almost worse than I feel," Vince said sympathetically. "I believe you, Liz. I'm sorry I doubted you. . . . I feel better knowing that you weren't behind this, but that doesn't really change things."

"What do you mean?" Elizabeth asked. Her stomach was in knots, and her heart was in her throat. It seemed to her that her whole world was

164

falling apart at once. *I'm not sure I can take any more bad news,* she thought miserably. *No, I know I can't take any more bad news.*

"I was hoping that as few people would see this show as possible, but now everybody and their dog will show up just so they can get an eyeful of 'hot,' 'hip' Vince Klee," Vince said bitterly. "I don't see any way out of this either, unless I jump off the Empire State Building."

"Well . . . that's an option," Elizabeth joked flatly. "If I had only known what Tom was up to—"

"It's not your fault." Vince sighed. "Listen, I've got to get ahold of my agent and talk some damage control. I'll catch up with you later. Bye."

Elizabeth hung up the phone and sat on the stool again. She folded her arms on the counter and laid down her head. *What's happened to my life?* she asked herself. *Everything was going so well at first, but now I feel like I've taken a wrong turn. When did things start turning rotten?*

She turned her head listlessly and looked at the shelves where Tish kept her herbal remedies. "Maybe Tish has something that will make me feel better," she muttered as she scanned the labels. "Peppermint tea for stomachaches, dried lavender for muscle aches . . . nope . . . nothing there for heartaches."

There was one good, old-fashioned remedy Elizabeth knew well. She put her head down again and settled in for a good, long cry.

*   *   *

165

The roar of the crowd was deafening, but Jessica could barely hear anything over the sound of her own blood pounding in her ears. She felt as tight as a harp string, and worry lines etched themselves across her brow. *This is it—the moment of reckoning!* she told herself for the tenth time in as many minutes.

Jessica glanced nervously around the gym. What had been a user-friendly workout room only the day before was now transformed into a chamber of horrors. Smoke filled the air—it seemed like every spectator present had taken up Sunshine's habit of smoking cigars—and the windows had been covered with black material. The workout mats had been piled against a far wall, and a makeshift ring had taken center stage. A male recruit in a black-and-white referee's shirt paced back and forth across the ring. To Jessica he looked like an executioner. Jessica shuddered, and her gaze strayed to the bottom of the ring. The mud-colored flooring looked stained with—

Blood, she noted grimly. *That's what it looks like, blood! And soon there'll be some more down there. Pure, priceless Wakefield blood courtesy of Vanessa T. Pruitt!* Jessica closed her eyes and tried to block out the scene.

"Stay loose, stay focused, stay loose, stay focused." Sunshine and Annette's rhythmic chanting provided a welcome distraction. Jessica leaned back against the ropes, trying to relax as

166

Bev massaged her shoulders and Annette loosened up her gloves.

It's no use, Jessica lamented. *I can't* relax! *For all I know, my friends aren't even my friends anymore! Who knows, maybe they're already plotting to sabotage me by spiking my water bottle or something.*

Jessica's eyes flew open at the thought, and she instantly wished they'd stayed shut. Pruitt, in golden satin trunks, was flashing her an evil grin from across the ring. Jessica stared in fascination at the frightening spectacle that Pruitt made. Her shoulders, accentuated by her black satin tank top, seemed sturdier than a lumberjack's. Her protective mouthpiece stretched her mouth out of all recognition, and the gleam in her eyes made her look insane.

"Not that she doesn't *always* look insane," Jessica muttered under her breath. "But that mouthpiece really—eeek! Where's my mouthpiece?" Jessica panicked.

"It's right here," Bev said soothingly as she handed it over to Jessica.

Jessica fumbled with her mouthpiece, trying to find the right bite. "This thing feels like a torture device," she mumbled, moving her jaw back and forth gingerly. When she was satisfied with how it felt, she punched her gloves together and shook them out to free up her nervous tension.

"Stay loose, stay focused," Sunshine and Annette continued reciting, but Jessica was tuned in to her own chant.

"Float like a butterfly, sting like a bee; float like a butterfly, sting like a bee." Jessica repeated Muhammad Ali's maxim to herself over and over. She knew that her greatest chance of survival lay not only in landing punches but in avoiding Pruitt's blows. "Float like a—"

Dingdingdingdingdingding!

Pruitt catapulted herself forward into the center of the ring, and Jessica moved to meet her tentatively, hopping back and forth on the balls of her feet. Pruitt feinted forward with a deadly left hook, but Jessica skipped aside, raising her gloves in front of her face protectively.

With a twist of her upper body and her elbows tight to her sides, Jessica managed to deflect a jab-cross combo from Pruitt. "All right," Jessica cheered herself on. "C'mon, float like a butterfly . . . duck!" She ducked a vicious right hook with barely an inch to spare. Jessica swallowed hard, still feeling the whiffle of Pruitt's punch.

The near miss seemed to inflame Pruitt; she grabbed Jessica in a bear hug and tightened her hold until Jessica could hardly breathe.

This is it! Jessica gasped, struggling to squirm out of Pruitt's clutches. She managed to free one elbow and jabbed Pruitt repeatedly in the abdomen. Unfortunately Pruitt didn't even seem to notice. *Is she made of* steel? Jessica wondered as stars began swimming in front of her eyes. *I'm . . . going . . . under. . . .*

"Ha! I knew you wouldn't be able to last with me." Pruitt squeezed Jessica tighter, her voice as fierce as her grip.

Wheeet!

Jessica looked around in confusion and saw the referee holding his whistle. "Break it up, break it up!" he shouted, separating the two of them while the crowd hooted and catcalled.

Not a moment too soon! Jessica thought as she circled Pruitt once more. *Block!* Jessica held her guard up to fend off an incoming blow. *Pivot!* She turned swiftly, causing Pruitt to nearly loose her balance. "I can do this!" Jessica crowed under her breath. "C'mon, float like a butterfly—"

"Talk to yourself much?" Pruitt asked in a menacing tone. "Gone crazy yet?" She circled Jessica like a hungry lioness out for blood.

Jessica had no time to think of a comeback; she was too busy avoiding a rapid series of right-left hooks. Fortunately, although Pruitt was as strong as a bull, she wasn't as nimble as Jessica, and she stumbled slightly as she tried to keep up with her.

"Ha! Who's having a hard time now?" Jessica sassed. "Not surprised. After all, not many guys take *you* out dancing at clubs, do they?" Jessica skipped backward with the grace of a ballerina and danced around the ring, evading an enraged Pruitt, who lumbered after her, swiping the air with herculean punches.

"When was the last time you went out on the

town, Pruitt?" Jessica asked as she neatly side-stepped a left hook. "Was it at a barn dance?" Jessica twirled away as Pruitt swung forward with an alternating jab-uppercut combination. Sweat poured down Jessica's face, but she continued to lead Pruitt in a merry dance around the ring.

"C'mon, Pruitt, try and catch me," Jessica taunted, although her breath was growing increasingly ragged. "I could always hop on one foot. I mean, knowing all the latest So-Cal club moves *is* an unfair advantage."

Yeah, right, Jessica thought dryly as she grooved around the perimeter of the ring. *As if having fists made of cement isn't!*

Her heart was beating so hard she thought it would burst, her breath came in shallow gasps, and her calves were burning with the effort required to stay on her toes.

Pruitt, on the other hand, seemed invincible. Although she hadn't been able to land a single punch, she didn't appear to be fatigued at all. In fact, if anything, Jessica's success only seemed to spur her on. Her eyes gleamed with a mad light as she pursued Jessica relentlessly. It was clear that she was trying to back Jessica into a corner.

"You'll never get *me* against the ropes!" Jessica promised, dancing toward the center.

Pruitt lurched after her, trying to land deadly jabs. Jessica feinted left, causing Pruitt's swing to fall wide.

Dingdingdingdingding!

Talk about saved by the bell! Jessica was giddy with relief. She tripped back to her corner and collapsed on the stool.

"Drink up." Annette passed Jessica a bottle of water. Jessica accepted it gratefully. She began gulping it down, too thirsty to wonder if it had been tampered with. She nearly moaned out loud as Sunshine kneaded the kinks out of her shoulders.

"You're doing great," Bev assured her, wiping her down with a towel.

Yeah, Jessica thought grimly. *I'm floating like a butterfly, all right. But unless I can start stinging like a bee, Pruitt's going to wipe the floor with me!*

Chapter Twelve

Lit beautifully, composed flawlessly, Tom thought as he sat in front of one of the monitors, sipping a cup of coffee as he viewed the final cut of his footage one last time. He had to admit that he'd done an excellent job. He deserved to be proud.

But I sure don't feel proud, he thought. *I feel like I'm a couple of rungs lower than Slimehog!* With a sigh Tom pushed his coffee away. He knew that he was drinking an expensive blend—Joey liked gourmet coffees—but right now the only thing that Tom could taste was his own bitterness.

What's going to happen when Elizabeth finds out I've lied to her? Tom groaned and covered his face with his hands. *If I could just make her understand that I only took this job out of desperation . . .* He lifted his head and stared mindlessly, glowering, at a torso shot of Vince Klee. *I only wanted her to respect me.*

Tom closed his eyes and allowed memory to wash over him. He thought back to how empty his life had been before Elizabeth had filled it with laughter and love. Tom hadn't even known that it was possible to care for someone as much as he did for Elizabeth. He hadn't known the joy of sharing his innermost thoughts with another person. And most of all, he hadn't known that another person could be more important to him than his own self. *I do know one thing, though,* Tom thought. *I know that I would rather die than hurt Elizabeth.*

He pushed back his chair and began pacing between the dubbing decks and editing tables. *How could I have gotten myself into a situation like this?* he asked himself angrily. *Elizabeth has so much integrity. I know that she would rather see me unemployed than work at a place like this.*

Tom pounded his fist on the editing table. Drawing himself up to his full height, he squared his shoulders and walked briskly out of the screening room toward Joey's office. Tom paused on the threshold of the office, unsure of how to begin, but Joey called out to him.

"Something on your mind, kid? Pull up a chair and tell Uncle Joey all about it."

Tom crossed the office in a few swift steps, his feet sinking into the lush pile of the carpet. He sighed for a moment, flashing back to the day he'd given up his internship at Action 5 News. Back then he'd known he was throwing away a great opportunity. Today he felt much different. "I'm really sorry, Joey," Tom began, clearing his throat. "I think the people here are really terrific, and you're a great producer—you can crank out a show better than anyone I've ever worked with, but—"

"This isn't the kind of stuff you had in mind when you came to the Big Apple, right?" Joey paused to take a sip of his coffee. "You thought you were going to get a job at one of the networks or dailies. You thought you would uncover some story that would get you nominated for the Pulitzer before you were even through with your summer vacation, right?"

Tom blushed. "Well, the truth is, I—"

"Forget it." Joey waved his hand expansively. "To be honest, I didn't think you'd last here."

"No?" Tom asked, startled. "Was there something wrong with my work?"

"Nah, you got me all wrong. I was giving you a *compliment*. You got class, ethics, that kind of stuff. This kind of gig isn't for everybody. Truth is"—Joey paused for a second and studied Tom shrewdly—"the truth is, you remind me of myself when I was young."

"Really?" Tom wasn't sure whether to be flattered or not.

"Yeah, I had integrity. Once. I wasn't always a producer of sleaze and tease." Joey looked down at his coffee and was uncharacteristically silent for a few moments. "Tell you what, kid. I'm going to help you out, make a couple calls. A friend of mine's got a magazine—"

Tom began to blush as he pictured just what kind of magazine Joey was talking about. *Let me guess,* he thought wryly. *It probably has a lot of pictures—*

"No, no, don't look like that," Joey interrupted his train of thought. "It's a first-class publication. He uses it as a tax write-off. Probably won't pay much, maybe nothing, but you'll get to write about intellectual stuff and use a lot of four-dollar words."

"Thank you," Tom said, surprised. His blood began to tingle as he imagined how fun it would be to sink his teeth into something challenging.

"Hey, no problem. I'll give you a call after I run this guy to the ground." Joey stood up and extended his hand across the desk. "Get out of here, Tommy. Go out there and change the world."

Tom grasped his hand, comforted by Joey's strong, firm grip. "Thanks a lot, Joey. And I meant what I said. You really do know how to get a show out."

"Yeah, yeah." Joey looked embarrassed. "See you around, kid."

Tom walked out of the office, his step a million times lighter than it had been just moments before.

He turned around to look at Joey once more. But Joey had his back to him and was staring out the window to the city below.

Well, that was a shock! Tom thought, shaking his head. *So Joey thinks that I have integrity, huh? I just hope Elizabeth feels the same way.*

How am I going to survive? Jessica asked herself. *I can't keep avoiding Pruitt forever. Sooner or later she's going to land a punch and* wham! *Bye-bye, Jessica! If I could . . .*

"Hey, what are you doing?" she asked Sunshine, distracted. "Why are you untying my gloves?"

"Your gloves are a little . . . tight," Sunshine replied smoothly.

"Oh, right." Jessica nodded. She wasn't quite sure what Sunshine was talking about. Loosening her gloves *sounded* like a good idea, but what did she know? Was it possible that this was a trick?

Jessica looked across the ring at Pruitt, trying to see how the prune-faced torture master was holding up. In response to her gaze Pruitt spit out her mouth guard and sneered. While sweat was dripping from Jessica's brow and she was flat-out panting, Pruitt's breathing was even, and she didn't appear to be sweating.

She looks like she could keep going forever, Jessica realized, her heart sinking in despair. *She looks like she could knock my—*

"What's that?" Jessica looked at Sunshine, who was continuing to fiddle with her gloves. Suddenly Jessica felt the sensation of cold metal against her palms. "Something just fell into my gloves," Jessica complained. "Eeew, get it out!"

"Shhh!" Bev looked around furtively.

"Oldest trick in the book, honey," Sunshine whispered in her ear.

"We all planned it together," Annette said under her breath as she pretended to fuss with Jessica's shoelaces.

They packed my punch with lead! Jessica realized, awed at the risk they were all taking. *I can fight now! I can even win! They are on my side, I guess. . . . Now I just have to go out there and—*

Dingdingdingdingding!

Jessica surged forward to the center of the ring. *You bet I'll sting like a bee now!* she thought with an inward cheer.

Pruitt's eyes widened in shock as Jessica came out swinging. She took advantage of Pruitt's surprise to land a swift jab-cross combo. Jessica laughed in triumph as she skipped backward to avoid Pruitt's retaliation.

"I was just faking you out before, Pruneface. Now you'll see what Jessica Wakefield is really made of!" Jessica punctuated her words with a series of right and left hooks. She felt a satisfying thud as her fist connected with Pruitt's jaw. Pruitt didn't fall, but she did sway, and Jessica followed up with a series of battering uppercuts that backed Pruitt against the ropes, where she was at Jessica's mercy.

"How does *that* feel?" Jessica growled as she landed punch after punch. All of Pruitt's insanely cruel treatment replayed itself in Jessica's mind as she pummeled Pruitt with her fists. "I never thought I'd enjoy hitting someone," Jessica seethed. "But I'm giving you what you *deserve*."

Jessica was dimly aware that the crowd was going wild. The spectators shouted and cheered, some of them calling out her name. But Jessica's focus was on Pruitt and Pruitt only. "Take that," Jessica cried, landing a blow to Pruitt's abdomen.

Pruitt bellowed like a bull and broke away from Jessica's onslaught. She moved sideways, ducking punches, but the blows she'd received made her footwork clumsier than ever.

"Now who's running scared?" Jessica called out as she stalked after Pruitt. The crowd outside the ring was a blur as she pursued Pruitt relentlessly around the ring.

"You just got lucky," Pruitt panted, biting her words off venomously. "Taking a punch from you is like being tickled with a feather duster."

"Is that so? Let's see how this one feels." Jessica swung out with a power-packed punch but missed.

"You're a joke, princess." Pruitt laughed through her mouth guard as she swung out with a series of killer punches.

"You can't get me!" Jessica sang out. She managed to fend off Pruitt's punches and land several more of her own. Pruitt looked dazed by Jessica's sudden show of strength, but even though she was taking hits, she wasn't down yet, and Jessica, although she was landing punches, was more tired than she wanted to admit.

"Think you can bring me down?" Pruitt hissed under her breath as she and Jessica circled each other. "You're out of your mind. I'm just playing with you, giving you a taste of victory before I waste you." She spat on the floor. "That's what I think of you, Wakefield."

"That does it," Jessica declared furiously. "I'm wiping the floor with you!" Anger fueled her with adrenaline as she followed up a right uppercut with a jab-cross combo. Pruitt deflected most of the blows and tried to hit back with a right hook, but her fist caught air.

"Faked you out, didn't I?" Jessica gloated as she easily skipped away from Pruitt's fists. Her one ambition in life was to wipe the malicious smile off Pruitt's face once and for all.

Jessica easily dodged a desperate jab. "Oops! Sorry, *sir*, you seem a little slow." Jessica landed a teasing right-cross punch across the bridge of Pruitt's nose. "Let's try again, shall we? See if you can avoid *this*." Jessica alternated right and left hooks to Pruitt's face and abdomen, sending her staggering backward. "Fall," Jessica shouted. "C'mon, fall!"

180

When Pruitt regained her footing—just barely—Jessica rained blows on Pruitt's head. Pruitt held up her gloves to ward them off.

"Gotcha!" Jessica exulted. With Pruitt's hands raised in a defensive position, Jessica lunged forward for the kill.

Right hook, left hook, uppercut to the stomach! Jessica chanted to herself. Pruitt put her gloves down to parry the punches, but she wasn't quick enough.

Right, left, right, left, right, left, right! The crack of Jessica's fist connecting with Pruitt's jaw was like thunder. Pruitt looked dazed. She rocked backward on her heels for a second and toppled to the floor in what appeared to be a dead faint.

"Ten . . . nine . . . eight . . ."

Dingdingdingdingding!

"Seven . . . six . . ."

The entire crowd counted down along with the referee, who was standing over Pruitt's still, moaning form.

Just stay down there, Jessica prayed. She saw Pruitt's eyelids flutter open. *No! Stay under!*

"Five . . . four . . ."

Pruitt stirred and tried to raise herself on one elbow.

Jessica clenched her fists, her brow puckered with anxiety. The suspense seemed even worse than the fight itself.

"Three . . ."

181

Pruitt sat halfway up.

No! Jessica closed her eyes, unable to look.

"Two . . ."

Pruitt stayed up for a second . . . and collapsed.

"One!" the referee bellowed, barely audible over the roar of the crowd. "The winner is Jessica Wakefield!" The referee held her hand high, and the gym erupted in a frenzy. She looked over at her friends, who were bouncing up and down and hugging each other wildly in her corner.

After the referee let her arm down, Jessica smiled through her tears as she waved at the cheering crowd. She turned to the referee to shake his hand, but he was no longer there. Instead she was shocked to see Commander Phipps, in full dress uniform, climbing into the ring.

I didn't know he was here! Jessica thought, her head spinning with excitement. *What, did he declare today an FSSA-wide holiday or something?*

"You have a great future, young lady," Commander Phipps boomed over the noise of the crowd as he clasped her arm. "I'm proud to have you here at FSSA. You're a credit to the rest of us!" He leaned in closer to Jessica. "And between you and me . . . Sergeant Pruitt had it coming," he added, his eyes twinkling.

Chapter Thirteen

"Having Tom betray me *isn't* the worst thing that could have happened," Elizabeth tried to convince herself as she sat on the couch in Tish's living room. "I mean, it would have been *much, much* worse if we'd slept together—and *then* he betrayed me!"

Somehow this realization failed to comfort Elizabeth, and she buried her head in her hands with a heartfelt sigh.

Usually just being in the warmth and comfort of Tish's apartment had the power to soothe her, but right now the apartment was failing to work its usual magic. So Elizabeth had turned to the one surefire cure she knew—her journal. But even *that* old standby wasn't working.

She stood up in frustration, tumbling her journal to the floor, and unconsciously twisted the gold bangle bracelet Tom had given her. Elizabeth noticed what she was doing and took off the bracelet. Turning it over in her hands, she read the inscription.

Elizabeth, I love you forever.

"Ha!" Elizabeth laughed sarcastically. "And just how long is forever, Tom?" she asked the empty living room. "Is *forever* until you get tired of waiting for me to sleep with you?"

Could that really be true? Elizabeth wondered as a tear made its way down her cheek. *Is this whole* Tease-n-Tell *fiasco Tom's way of lashing out at me because we didn't make love?*

Elizabeth rocked back and forth, overcome by a torrent of conflicting feelings. Elizabeth was deeply wounded by Tom's actions, but she couldn't allow herself to believe that her unwillingness to have sex was acceptable justification for Tom's behavior. In fact, if that really was the case, that made him more despicable than ever. Still, Elizabeth couldn't help wondering how things would have turned out if they had slept together—on Monday, Tuesday, Wednesday. . . .

"Should we have done it after all?" she asked herself. "Would it have been so wrong?"

She sat back down and took herself back to those nights that seemed so full of possibilities. *What would it have felt like?* she wondered. *What would we be doing right now? Would we be snuggled up in bed instead of at each other's throats?*

Elizabeth closed her eyes and tried to picture

the scene. She thought of how exciting Tom's kisses could be, how his hands would feel on her body, so warm and strong. *Would the rest of it be even more exciting?* she mused, allowing herself to delve deeper into the fantasy. In her mind she was wrapped in Tom's arms and feeling his love, becoming one with him. *Was I wrong to deny myself that pleasure?* She could almost imagine how wonderful it would be, how vulnerable she would feel. . . .

Elizabeth's eyes snapped open. "That's right, I'd be vulnerable," she said bitterly. "I was *right* not to sleep with Tom. After what I saw today, how could I trust him?" Elizabeth shook her head as humiliating feelings of betrayal surged through her. "What am I *thinking?* The kind of man that I could trust enough to sleep with is *not* the kind of man who would behave the way Tom has!"

Elizabeth froze as she heard the sound of the door opening. Tish had driven to upstate New York to go mushroom hunting, and Elizabeth knew she wouldn't be back for several hours. Only one other person she knew of could be coming through that door.

Swallowing hard, Elizabeth tried to quell the different sensations swirling through her body. On the one hand, the thought of confronting Tom with her anger raised anxious goose bumps on her arms. But the *other* fantasies she'd been entertaining were having a *very* different effect on her.

Elizabeth braced herself. She could hear Tom's footsteps in the foyer. She took a deep breath and whirled around just as Tom appeared around the corner, a sheepish expression on his face.

The sheepish expression was all she needed to set her in motion. "How could you *do* such a thing?" Elizabeth raged before Tom had a chance to open his mouth. Her eyes shot fiery sparks. "Just tell me one thing," she began, her voice quivering with anger and worry. "Did you do this because we didn't make love?"

"How could you think that?" Tom cried, his voice raw with pain.

"How could I think that?" she repeated incredulously. "*Maybe* because you lied to me! *Maybe* because you betrayed me!"

"Elizabeth, I never meant to betray you." Tom's face was deathly pale. He made a move toward Elizabeth, but she backed away from him. "Things just seemed to get out of hand. I was so desperate to get a job that I was afraid to say no to the assignment. But Elizabeth, you have to believe me. I was miserable about the whole thing."

"Oh, really?" Elizabeth's voice was rich with sarcasm. "*You* were miserable? How do you think *I* feel? How do you think *Vince* feels?"

Tom hung his head. "I can imagine," he said quietly. "Look, if it makes you feel any better, I just quit *Tease-n-Tell*."

"You what?" Elizabeth asked savagely. "You

quit your 'classy cable newsmagazine currently in development'?"

Tom winced. It was clear that Elizabeth's words wounded him deeply. "I just couldn't stay with the show, Elizabeth."

"Great," Elizabeth said furiously. "I'm glad your sense of ethics isn't on a permanent vacation, but did it have to wait *this* long to resurface? It seems awfully convenient for you to start feeling bad *now.*" She spun away from Tom, clutching her stomach. She'd been so sure that getting things off her chest would help her, but now she was in more pain than ever. She felt the warmth of Tom's presence behind her.

"Let me make it up to you," he begged softly. "Please listen to my apologies. And please, *please* don't think I did this because we didn't sleep together." She felt his arms reach out for her.

"Don't." Elizabeth moved away and watched him warily. "Don't just think that you can kiss and make up this time, Tom." Tears brimmed in Elizabeth's eyes, but she blinked them back. "You *lied* to me. You took my trust and you threw it away." Her voice broke on the word *trust,* and the tears returned.

"Don't you think I know that, Elizabeth?" Tom sighed raggedly and ran a hand through his hair. "Don't you think that I'm eating myself alive over this? Look, I quit so that—"

"*Quit?*" Elizabeth threw the word back in his

187

face. "You mean after selling me and Vince down the river, you didn't even have the courage to stick it out? This whole time in New York you've been moping around without a job, and now that you have one, you walk away!" She shook her head in disbelief.

Tom's mouth hung open for a moment. "I don't get it, Elizabeth," he finally said, breaking the deafening silence. "I can't believe you'd still want me to work for that show."

Elizabeth looked at her boyfriend as if he were a stranger. "No, Tom," she began softly. "You don't get it, do you? What I *want*," she cried, "is to have a boyfriend who doesn't *lie* to me! I want a boyfriend who won't betray me—or my friends!" She whipped her head away and began stalking back and forth on the Oriental rug.

Tom cleared his throat. "Did it ever occur to you that I wouldn't even have *taken* the lousy job if you hadn't made it abundantly clear that you thought I was fast becoming a loser?" His voice was deadly quiet and laced with pain.

"Take responsibility for your own actions, Tom," Elizabeth snapped. "It's not *my* fault that you did this to me and Vince."

Rolling his eyes, Tom held out his hands in a futile gesture. "Oh, I am so *sick* and *tired* of hearing about *Vince!* Vince, Vince, *Vince!*" He seemed to recoil as Vince's name hung in the air. "You know something? I'm *glad Tease-n-Tell* trashed the guy!"

Elizabeth gasped. She flinched, unable to withstand the force of the disgust and anguish in Tom's brown eyes.

"You hear me? *Glad!*" Tom repeated before he stormed out of the living room.

Elizabeth jumped slightly at the crash his bedroom door made as he slammed it shut. Tears flowing down her face, she flung herself down on the couch in utter misery and hugged a pillow for comfort. *I have no one to talk to,* she realized with a sob. *Not Tish, not anybody. Not even Jessica—*

Jessica! Elizabeth sat bolt upright, her tears suddenly forgotten as she raced to the kitchen and hurriedly punched in the number of FSSA. *C'mon, pick up, pick up!* Elizabeth prayed, her heart in her throat as she wiped at her face with her sleeve. She counted twenty rings before she realized that *nobody* was there to pick up. Slowly she hung up the phone and closed her eyes in terror, trying to block out the frightening images that were flashing before her. *She's got to be OK,* she assured herself. *She just has to. If something horrible happened, I would have felt it. But still . . .*

"Who can I talk to?" Elizabeth asked the phone tearfully. "Who can help me? I just need a friendly shoulder; I just need—"

Vince.

Her fingers trembling, Elizabeth picked up the receiver and began to dial.

*　　　*　　　*

"It was awesome," Jessica admitted to her fellow recruits between swigs of mess hall apple juice. "Totally. I knew I'd have Pruitt eating the mat in no time."

Sunshine chuckled. "Too bad we don't have anything better to celebrate with than flat club soda, warm apple juice, and stale crackers," she apologized. "I mean, you're a *winner*, Jessica. You deserve better than this!"

"Forget it," Jessica replied, giddy with relief. "Right now I'm just so happy to be alive and in one piece that even warm apple juice tastes great to me." She knocked back her glass and emptied it. "I mean it," Jessica continued. "You think Pruitt looks scary? Wait until you see her coming at you across a boxing ring. If she wore that mouth guard on Halloween, she'd win first prize, no problem."

"I can imagine." One of the recruits, a petite brunette, shuddered. "But honestly, you were incredible. I thought for sure Pruitt was going to murder you!"

"Gee, thanks for the vote of confidence."

"Oh, hey, I didn't mean—"

"Kidding," Jessica replied with a laugh as she adjusted the white terry robe around her shoulders. "I had everything under control." She winked at Sunshine and smiled at Bev and Annette, who were busy trying out the Wakefield Boxstep in the corner.

"So how did you figure out your strategy, Jessica?" another recruit, a tall, thin blonde, asked. "Your footwork was incredible!"

"That's just Jessica's So-Cal dance style," Sunshine interjected. "She trained in all the best nightclubs."

"Yeah—it's pretty hard too." Annette wiped a few unruly dark curls away from her forehead and returned to the table, with Bev bopping merrily behind.

Jessica shrugged modestly and passed her mug to Sunshine for a refill. *I always knew that going out dancing was much more important than studying,* she mused, *but I never dreamed it would pay off like this!*

"What do you think is going to happen to Pruitt now?" Annette asked. "Do you think she'll have to take a leave of absence?"

A loud cheer followed the question.

"Now, now, let's not be catty," Bev admonished. "I think Pruitt has suffered enough punishment for a while."

"Speech, Jessica, speech!" Sunshine cried out.

Annette and Bev took up the chant, and soon the whole party joined in, banging their tin mugs on the table.

Jessica held up her hand. "Well . . . I couldn't. I really couldn't. . . . It wouldn't be right," she protested, completely enthralled with the idea.

"Go on, Jess," Bev called out.

"OK, if you insist," Jessica said quickly. She climbed onto the table as her fellow barrack mates dissolved in laughter.

Jessica rolled up her napkin and held it in front of her face like a microphone. "First of all, I'd like to thank everyone who . . ." She trailed off as an officer entered the mess hall. Everyone immediately snapped to attention.

"Jessica Wakefield," the officer announced gravely. "You, Sunshine Harris, Annette Polanco, and Beverly Vernon are to report to Commander Phipps's office on the double." He saluted smartly and turned on his heel.

What's this about? Jessica wondered as she put down her microphone, intrigued. *I bet Commander Phipps is going to give me an award or something! A ribbon or two would be just the thing to perk up the FSSA jumpsuit. . . .*

Jessica climbed down from the table and smiled brightly at her friends, but she couldn't help noticing that Sunshine and Co. were looking thoroughly confused.

"C'mon," Jessica said confidently. She linked arms with Sunshine, Bev, and Annette and swaggered out of the mess hall. *I can't wait to see what Commander Phipps has in store for me,* she thought excitedly. *Maybe it won't be a ribbon. Maybe it will be something gold . . . yeah, solid gold!*

* * *

"Central Park may not be the California coast-line, but I think it's pretty special. What about you?" Vince waved his hand to include the sweeping green lawns and flowering trees.

"It's beautiful." Elizabeth adjusted her baseball cap and looked around her as they strolled through an arcade of weeping willows. The breeze stirred the branches gracefully, and the air was soft and warm. Elizabeth could glimpse, through the lacy patterns of the leaves, an old-fashioned horse drawn carriage; the *clip-clop* of the horse's hooves was the only noise around.

"I can hardly believe we're standing right in the middle of Manhattan," she breathed in awe. "I haven't really explored the park that much. What a good idea to meet here." Elizabeth glanced shyly at Vince. Calling him had seemed like the thing to do at the time, but now she was feeling more than a little bashful.

"I'm glad you called," Vince said warmly. "I've wanted to get together with you outside of the theater, and I really wanted to take a walk in the park with you someday. So . . ."

". . . here we are."

Vince smiled softly and paused next to an exquisite ornate fountain. "This is Bethesda Fountain. I think it's a required location shot for every love story set in New York. I know—I did a movie here last year. It was at night, and the whole thing was lit up."

"It sounds romantic," Elizabeth said. *It certainly looks it too,* she thought, her cheeks warm.

"Would you like to get something to drink?" Vince gestured to an outdoor café a few yards away.

"Sure." Elizabeth sat down in a wrought iron chair he pulled out for her and looked around with pleasure. The splashing sprays of water that poured out of the fountain made a lovely sound, and every table boasted a vase with a spray of white roses. She and Vince sat in companionable silence for a few minutes before a waitress approached.

"Lemonade OK?" Vince quirked his eyebrows at her.

"Perfect." Elizabeth nodded. "So, I haven't asked you lately. How are your rehearsals going. . . ." She trailed off as the waitress returned with their drinks. Elizabeth chewed on the sprig of mint that adorned the old-fashioned frosted glass and looked at Vince expectantly.

"Well . . ." Vince paused for a second as if he were gathering his courage. "I'm going to walk, Elizabeth. I know that sounds cowardly, but I just can't go through with it." Vince took a long swallow of his lemonade. "I thought that maybe things would come together, you know, shape up somehow, but opening night's not too far off, and things only seem to be getting worse."

"Vince, I don't think that you're cowardly at all," Elizabeth assured him. She surprised herself by reaching across the table to take his hand, and her heart did a small somersault at the look Vince gave her in response. "I think you've been incredibly brave. I mean, you didn't know when you started that you were getting involved with nudity—"

"And pretentiousness," Vince added.

"And all that nonsense," Elizabeth finished, averting her eyes. "The situation is totally unfair to you. You deserve better."

"Thanks, Elizabeth." Vince squeezed her hand. "Your opinion really means a lot to me."

She looked up to see his dark eyes gazing deep into hers. She tore her eyes away, embarrassed by his intense scrutiny, and fiddled with her straw instead. "Anyway, I think it's great that you're standing up for yourself. You came to New York to get some real stage experience, not to star in a peep show!"

"Thanks to you, Liz, I *am* going to stand up for myself," Vince said heartily. "In fact, I'm going to 'stand up' right now!" He pushed back his chair with a grin.

"Where are you . . . going. . . ." Elizabeth trailed off in amazement as Vince shucked his leather jacket and spun it around as if he were auditioning for a sequel to *The Full Monty*. With a sly wink he began dancing around their table, humming an insanely tuneless song and executing some unbelievably sexy moves. All the while his mischievous grin never left his face.

"Ba-da-baaaa," he sang as he unbuttoned his vintage short-sleeve bowling shirt to reveal a thin white T-shirt underneath. "Ba-da-baaa-doo-da-doo-boo-dee-doop-doo . . ."

"Vince!" Elizabeth blurted, her face as red as a tomato. "What are you *doing?*" She brought her hands up to her face in astonishment, taking her eyes off him long enough to glance around the café in case anyone else was observing Vince's gyrations. Thankfully the few other patrons went about their business as if male strippers entertained the clientele every day.

"Don't you see, Elizabeth?" Vince asked as he boogied around her chair and made kissy faces. "You hit the nail on the head! I'm *not* getting real theater experience. The only thing I'm learning from Claire's play is how to be a . . . a cheap piece of meat!"

Elizabeth burst into peals of laughter. "You're crazy, Vince."

"Crazy about yooo-ooou," Vince crooned as he extended his hand toward her.

"Oh yeah," Elizabeth joked, then hesitated. *Is he serious?* she wondered, studying his face closely. The playful smile was still there, but there was something shining in his eyes—something deep and mystifying. *I'm misreading things,* she told herself. *Vince isn't interested in* me. *I'm just*—

"Let's dance," Vince sang.

Before Elizabeth could protest, Vince had pulled her to her feet and was twirling her around in his arms. She let herself be swept away as they spun around Bethesda Fountain; the willow trees whispered, the fountain water splashed, providing the perfect musical accompaniment to their waltz. Elizabeth was naturally graceful, and even though she was in overalls and a baseball cap, she felt like a princess.

I can't believe I'm doing this, Elizabeth thought as she stared into Vince's dark eyes. *And yet* . . . Vince's hold on her tightened, and he returned her gaze with a passion that shook her.

"Elizabeth," Vince murmured as he slowed their pace. "Oh, Elizabeth." Vince bent his head close to hers as they tumbled down onto the nearby grass.

Vince cradled Elizabeth's face gently between his palms. Elizabeth lay still, breathless from their dizzying waltz and paralyzed by wonder. She was mesmerized by the passion that flowed from him. She felt protected by his strong, masculine arms.

"I've wanted to do this for so long," Vince said as he covered her mouth with his own.

Elizabeth allowed herself to be caught up in the magic of the kiss. Vince's arms tightened around her, and Elizabeth returned the pressure of his mouth with her own. *This feels incredible. This feels spectacular. This feels . . .*

Wrong! Guiltily Elizabeth held back a gasp and pushed Vince away. "I'm sorry, Vince," she said hastily as she sat up and brushed grass from her hair. "I'm really, really sorry. Believe me, I wish . . . I don't know—I just can't do this." Elizabeth looked down at the slender gold bangle on her wrist with a bittersweet smile. "No matter how angry I am at Tom, I still love him. I love him way too much to do something like this." Elizabeth paused and looked at Vince, her blue-green eyes pleading. "Believe me, if I wasn't with Tom . . ." She shrugged helplessly.

"I get the picture." Vince sighed ruefully. He smiled as he helped Elizabeth pull the grass out of her hair. "So . . . you wouldn't happen to have an identical twin or anything, do you?" he asked jokingly.

Jessica! All of Elizabeth's earlier anxieties came flooding back in an instant. The warmth from Vince's embrace evaporated as if it had never been. Elizabeth's heart hammered against her ribs in fear. *I've got to call Jessica!*

"Actually, Vince—I do," she choked out.

His eyes widened. "You do? Well, hey," he began in a joking tone. "Maybe—"

"And for all I know, she's mincemeat right now!" Elizabeth cried as she scrambled to her feet. "I've got to get home! I've got to call her!" Elizabeth sprinted away, leaving Vince speechless as she ran across the grass. *I just hope that I'm not too late,* she thought grimly, regretting the thought the instant it formed.

Chapter Fourteen

If Commander Phipps offers me a choice, I'll take a ribbon, Jessica mused as she and her gal pals marched into Commander Phipps's office. *Gold is better, but a medal might be too chunky to pin on some of my evening dresses. But ribbons would pretty much go with everything!* She stopped in front of Commander Phipps's desk and saluted smartly, a huge smile on her face.

"Sit down," Commander Phipps demanded gravely.

Jessica looked at him in surprise. *Why does he sound so serious?* she wondered. She glanced at her friends in confusion, but they appeared as baffled as she was. Mutely Jessica sat down.

Commander Phipps stared at the four of them for a few minutes before he reached into his desk drawer and removed Jessica's boxing gloves. Without a word he tossed them on his blotter.

Jessica gasped in dismay at the sight of them. Her heart sank as she watched Phipps casually remove the lead from within the mitts.

"It seems that my good wishes for your future were a little premature, Ms. Wakefield," he said sternly. "I had intended to call the recruiters at Star Watchers before they came and give you my full endorsement. Fortunately before I could make the call"—he paused, scowling—"an unnamed source revealed just how you won such a stunning victory." He picked up the lead and held it in his hands, shaking his head sorrowfully. "Moreover, I was informed that you didn't act alone in this matter." He shot baleful looks at Sunshine, Bev, and Annette, who all paled visibly under his glare.

What happens now? Jessica thought, clutching her stomach. *Whatever it is, I just hope it doesn't involve cleaning toilets again.*

"The security business has to fight against a lot of misconceptions," Commander Phipps said as he put the lead pieces back on his desk. "People think it's full of misfits, cheats, and liars. But I've worked hard to make sure that FSSA is seen differently. We have a strong reputation." He paused and gave each of them a searching glance. "That reputation is not served by having cheaters in our midst. I'm expelling all of you, dishonorably."

Jessica's jaw dropped open. Sunshine gasped, and Annette and Bev looked as if they'd just gone fifteen rounds with Pruitt.

"You'll be given enough time to get your effects in order," Phipps continued, "and then you'll be escorted to the airport."

Jessica felt as if her world had ended. *I can't just be expelled!* she thought in agony. *I'll never get over the shame!* "I . . . I . . . ," Jessica stammered, too numbed by shock.

"You can't expel us, sir," Bev exclaimed.

"That's right." Sunshine nodded in agreement. "Pruitt was out to get Jessica. There was nothing else that Jessica could have done to save herself."

"We were just trying to help," Annette spoke up. "If we hadn't loaded Jessica's gloves, she would have gotten killed!"

"What else could we have done?" Jessica finally managed to croak out. "I had no choice. I'm just glad that my friends were able to help me."

"But you *did* have a choice, Jessica." Commander Phipps regarded her severely. "You could have chosen *not* to fight. You could have come to me before you took the law into your own hands. I'm afraid you used very poor judgment, Ms. Wakefield." Commander Phipps pushed his chair back from the desk and stood up. "Being able to think situations through in a calm, rational manner is an essential part of being a security agent, and that, as much as the fact that you were dishonest, is why I'm expelling all four of you. Dismissed."

Jessica looked to her friends for comfort, but

they were as ashen faced as she was. *It looks like Pruitt won after all,* she realized bitterly as she stumbled to her feet and staggered out the door.

"I can't remember the last time I felt this bad," Tom muttered as he lay in bed and stared up at the ceiling. The ceiling in his bedroom was very pretty, painted all over with the constellations in silver against a midnight blue background. But after four hours Tom was growing bored with it.

He'd been in the same position ever since he'd slammed the door to his room. He thought that he might stay that way a little longer. "In fact," Tom mumbled unhappily, "I might never get up again."

He could hear Tish busily puttering around the kitchen, but the rest of the apartment was quiet. Much too quiet. Tom knew that he and Tish were alone in the apartment. *Which means that Elizabeth is still out! Now, let's see, buddy, where could she be?* Tom asked himself sarcastically. *Could she be with all the people that we know in New York? No, because we don't know anyone here! Could she be at the Maxwell? No, because it's closed today. Could she be with Vince Klee? Dingdingding! You win first prize!*

Tom punched the pillows in frustration. *If she breaks up with me, that's not the worst part—no, sirree,* Tom thought, shaking his head. *The worst part is that everything she said was* right!

He rolled off the bed and walked over to the mirror. "What's happened to me?" he asked his reflection quietly. "Why did I take that stupid job to begin with?" His reflection stared sadly back at him, unable to answer.

Tom paced back and forth, thinking about how his life had become such an utter fiasco. *I thought that if Liz and I were together, we'd have the best summer ever,* he lamented. *I thought that Elizabeth and I would reach a new level in our relationship. I thought that we would finally make love. . . .*

He eyed the empty bed wistfully, envisioning how Elizabeth would look wrapped up in his blankets, his arms, and nothing else. He swallowed hard and turned away.

There was a soft knock on the door. *Elizabeth!* Tom's heart thudded against his ribs, and for a moment he couldn't speak.

"Tom? Are you all right?"

Tom's spirits sank as he recognized Tish's voice.

"I haven't heard a peep out of you in hours."

Tom crossed the room to open the door. "Hi, Tish." He summoned up a smile in response to her look of motherly concern.

"Is anything wrong?" she asked, her bracelets jangling as she pushed back her hair. "Where's Elizabeth?"

Flying to Paris—with Vince Klee. Going to the Bahamas—with Vince Klee. Winning an Oscar—

with Vince Klee. I don't know where she is; I just know that she's with Vince Klee!

"I guess she's out. How was mushroom hunting?" Tom asked, anxious to change the subject.

Tish studied him shrewdly. "Why don't you come into the kitchen with me while I stew the mushrooms. We can have a little snack and chat." She took Tom by the hand as if he were a little boy and led him into the cheerful kitchen.

Tom slumped down on one of the stools that Tish had drawn up to the work island. "Let's see how you feel after some of this gets in you," Tish said kindly. She placed a cheerful pottery plate with several slabs of gingerbread dusted with sugar and topped with whipped cream in front of Tom.

"Is this some kind of herbal remedy?"

Tish smiled warmly and joined Tom on one of the other stools. "I think gingerbread is just one of those old-fashioned comforts, like chicken soup."

Tom nodded as he spooned into the warm gingerbread. It wasn't making his problems go away, but it *was* awfully soothing. He was about to compliment Tish on what a terrific cook she was when the phone rang.

"No, let me," Tom said as he saw Tish rise from her stool. "You probably need to relax after all that mushroom hunting." Tom wiped his mouth as he walked over to the phone and picked up the receiver.

"Tom?" a familiar voice shrieked. "I need Elizabeth!"

"Jessica? Are you all right?"

"I just want to talk to my sister!" she wailed.

"She's not here right now," Tom said gently. Although the connection was scratchy and it was slightly hard to make out Jessica's garbled words, there was no mistaking the fact that she was crying. "As soon as she gets in—"

"She can't call me!" Jessica sobbed on the other end. "She can't call me because I won't be here!"

"Jess, can I do anything?" Tom said, but the line was dead.

A flicker of fear touched Tom's heart as he replaced the receiver. He'd had his disagreements with Jessica in the past, but she was the twin sister of the woman that he loved, and he cared about her very much.

What happened? he asked himself, puzzled. *And how, after everything else Elizabeth's been through today, am I going to tell her about this?*

Elizabeth raced along the broad boulevards of Manhattan's Upper West Side. For once she was totally oblivious to her surroundings. She was so caught up in her worry for Jessica that she wouldn't have noticed if a herd of elephants paraded by.

She could still feel the pressure of Vince's lips

against her own. She could still feel how he had held her when they danced. She could still feel her earlier rage at Tom and her guilt at kissing Vince back. But all of those things faded in importance, and the only thought that hammered in her head was that she would die if anything had happened to Jessica.

Please let Jessica be all right, Elizabeth prayed over and over again as she hurried across the long crosstown blocks separating Central Park from Riverside Drive.

Elizabeth ran all the way to the building, and after fumbling for a second with her key, she flung herself through the foyer doors, into the elevator, and out to Tish's door. In a flash she'd whisked it open and charged into the kitchen, where Tom was sitting alone, eating a plate of gingerbread. Elizabeth barely noticed him as she lunged for the phone, panting.

"Jessica called for you," Tom announced before she had time to dial.

Elizabeth turned around, troubled by the concern in his voice. "Was she OK?" Elizabeth gasped out, pushing everything that had happened up until this point aside. She stared at him, her chest heaving, sweat dripping down her brow. She whipped off her baseball cap and wiped her forehead absentmindedly as she struggled to catch her breath.

"She didn't sound too good," Tom admitted

reluctantly. "She said that you probably wouldn't be able to reach her. But we just spoke a few minutes ago, so I'm sure you'll be able to get ahold of her." He stood up and walked tentatively toward Elizabeth with an expression of concern on his face.

Elizabeth paled visibly at his words and frantically dialed the number for FSSA. She was dimly aware that Tom was standing behind her and had placed his hand on her shoulder. Scared and anxious, she relaxed against Tom's body, allowing his strength to flow into her, infusing her with warmth and security.

"FSSA," a no-nonsense female voice barked out.

"Hello? This is Elizabeth Wakefield. I'm calling for my sister, Jessica Wakefield. She's—"

"She's no longer an FSSA trainee," the voice said flatly.

"Excuse me?" Elizabeth shook her head as if she couldn't believe what she was hearing. "I think there must be some mistake—"

"No mistake. This is Sergeant Pruitt. I was her drill sergeant, and believe me, I know. Wakefield was dismissed. *Dismissed*," she repeated, as if it gave her pleasure to say the word.

"Why?" Elizabeth cried out in shock. "What happened? Was she hurt? *You're* the one who should know!" Elizabeth's head was spinning so fast that she knew that if Tom weren't supporting her, she would collapse on the tiled floor. Anger bubbled up inside her. "Tell me *now!* You have no right to—"

"I'm not at liberty to divulge any more information," Pruitt snapped.

Elizabeth recoiled and stared at the phone as if it were a snake. The woman's voice had been about as gentle as a whiplash. *I can't believe Jessica fought this woman. If her voice sounds this bad, what must her punch be like?* Elizabeth wondered, her heart plummeting.

"Don't you dare hold out on me," she persisted. "Was my sister hurt during the boxing match? Is that why she's no longer there? Is she in the hospital?" Elizabeth's voice broke as pictures of a bandaged and injured Jessica swirled before her eyes. "Tell me, please!" she demanded. But the only response was the insistent buzzing of the dial tone. Pruitt had hung up.

Elizabeth slowly replaced the receiver. She turned to face Tom, tears streaming slowly down her face. "Something's happened to Jessica. She's been dismissed from FSSA!" Elizabeth whispered. "Oh, Tom, what can I do?"

"Are you sure that she was dismissed? Maybe she left voluntarily," Tom said in a soothing voice.

Elizabeth gazed up at Tom, hopelessness clouding her lovely face. "Oh, Tom, you know Jess—whatever happened, it isn't good! I'm so frightened. . . ."

Something horrible happened to Jess, she realized. *Something horrible happened to her, and I wasn't there to help. I didn't even get a chance to talk to her before—*

Elizabeth buried her head in her hands and sobbed.

It hurts so much to see Elizabeth so unhappy! Tom thought, his heart contracting painfully as he looked at Elizabeth. She stood with her back to him; her slim shoulders shook with the force of her tears. She looked so vulnerable. *I just want to wrap her in my arms and make everything better,* Tom thought. *But I don't know if Elizabeth wants any comfort from me right now.*

A flood of guilt engulfed Tom as he realized how much he had added to Elizabeth's problems. He stood uncertainly for a second and then moved behind her as she stood at the window.

"I'm so, so sorry . . . for everything," Tom murmured against her hair as he gathered her in his warm embrace. "You may not want to hear this right now, Elizabeth," he continued softly as he showered kisses down on her golden hair, "but I'm sorry for all the pain I caused you. I never meant to betray your trust, and I'll do anything to make it up to you."

Hey, I can *help out,* Tom realized. *It's not as if I have a job to go to tomorrow.* Tom turned Elizabeth around so that he could look in her face. "I'll fly to Miami," he told her. "I'll fly down there and find out what's going on with Jess. I'll take care of her, Elizabeth."

Elizabeth stared searchingly at Tom. Tears shimmered in her beautiful blue-green eyes. "Would you really do that for me, Tom?" she asked quietly.

"It would be my pleasure," Tom replied gravely. He gently wiped away the tears that trembled like crystal raindrops on the tips of her lashes. "You know I would do anything for you. I was so afraid . . . so afraid that I was going to lose you."

"Oh, Tom." Elizabeth rested her head against his broad chest. "You could never lose me."

Tom smiled contentedly as he rested his chin on her head. "I meant what I said about Jess, Elizabeth. There's nothing to keep me in the city right now. I can hop a plane and be there in a handful of hours."

"I'd be so happy if you did, Tom," Elizabeth said. "In fact, I think I should come with you."

"Are you serious?" Tom pulled away from her in shock. "What about your work here? What about the play?"

"None of that matters right now," Elizabeth said firmly. "Even if the play weren't going so badly, I'd want to come with you. Jessica is more important to me than all of this."

Tom nodded thoughtfully. "I guess I should have expected that from you," he said with a sad smile that crinkled the corners of his brown eyes. He reluctantly released Elizabeth from his embrace and pulled the phone book toward him. "We'll go down together." He began flipping through the yellow pages. "I'm going to call the airlines and book us on the next flight to Miami. You just relax—I'll take care of everything, and this whole mess will be behind us before you know it." Tom smiled at Elizabeth as he jotted down a few phone numbers. Despite the horrible circumstances surrounding them, he somehow suddenly felt the best he had since setting foot on New York soil.

"I'm afraid that's not good enough," Tom said authoritatively. "I need two tickets for tomorrow morning, nonstop to Miami. I'm sure if you check the computer again, you'll find two available seats. I'd be very surprised if everything is sold out. It's *not* a holiday weekend." He jotted some notes down on a pad in front of him. "Mm-hmm . . . yes, I thought so."

Elizabeth dried her eyes and nibbled the leftover gingerbread on Tom's plate. *It's such a relief to see Tom take charge,* she thought as she licked some whipped cream off her finger. The thought of being put on hold or dealing with reservation clerks in her present state was so unpleasant that she had almost cried in relief when Tom announced that he was taking care of everything.

She gazed at her boyfriend as his brow creased in thought, the phone tucked under his chin and his credit card in his hand. *How could I ever have thought he was losing it?* she asked herself. *Why, because he lost the heel from his shoe and was freaked out by some weirdo named Krull?*

"All right, so I have two confirmed reservations on flight CA three-two-four tomorrow morning at ten, leaving La Guardia Airport, correct?" Tom verified the tickets and hung up the phone. "Well, that's set," he announced as he looked up a number and quickly redialed.

"Who are you calling now?" Elizabeth queried.

"Car service." Tom sat down on one of the stools and kissed some gingerbread crumbs off Elizabeth's mouth. "We'll be leaving fairly early, and I don't want to have to deal with the hassle of getting a cab."

Elizabeth looked at her kind, handsome boyfriend with more appreciation than she had in weeks. Seeing the way he came together in a crisis made her remember why she loved him so much. *How could I have doubted him for a second?* she wondered mistily.

"Well, that's taken care of." Tom hung up the phone and smiled, laughing as Elizabeth lunged forward in a hug that sent them both toppling to the floor. "Hey, what's all this?" he asked teasingly as he wrapped his arms around Elizabeth, who was lying comfortably on top of him. "Hmmm . . . not that I mind." He kissed her deeply and gazed at her with a force that was overwhelming.

"I just love you, that's all." Elizabeth's sea green eyes glowed as she bent her head to kiss him again. Their lips fused together magically, and Elizabeth shivered in excitement. Tom's hands traced tingling paths along her back as he caressed her. Elizabeth plunged her hands into his dark hair as she broke away from his mouth to kiss his neck.

When they came up for air, Tom tucked a strand of her satiny hair behind her ear. "Seriously, though," he began quietly. "For a while it seemed like you were getting pretty friendly with old Vince Klee. He *is* an awfully good-looking guy. . . ."

Have his eyes ever looked so vulnerable? Elizabeth wondered as she swallowed down a lump in her throat. *Tom's right. Vince* is *an awfully good-looking guy and an awfully nice guy . . . but that doesn't make him Tom!*

Guilt coursed through her veins as the scene in Central Park flashed before her, and she looked away briefly. *What was I thinking, kissing Vince like that?* she asked herself incredulously. *I guess I've just been so confused lately, I didn't know where to turn. I know one thing for sure—kissing Vince was nothing like kissing Tom.*

"Vince is just a friend." Elizabeth smoothed her hand down the side of his cheek as she looked deeply into his questioning brown eyes. "You're my *best* friend, my soul mate, my *boyfriend*." She didn't know if all the love she felt for him was spilling out and bathing him in healing tenderness. She did know, however, that she had never felt about anyone the way she did about him.

"In that case," Tom said huskily, "do you think we can get up off this floor? The tiles are awfully cold, and there *is* a nice warm bed in the other room."

Does he mean what I think he does? Elizabeth wondered, wavering between feelings of excitement and nervousness. *Would this finally be the right time? Maybe it is. . . .*

"Hey." Tom touched her cheek. "I didn't mean it to sound like . . . well, you know, like I was pressuring you. I just meant that there were more comfortable places. . . ."

Elizabeth felt a small twinge of disappointment, but she laughed as she scrambled to her feet. "I know what you meant, Tom." She held out her hand with a smile and led the way to her bedroom.

"Who has the M&M's?" Bev asked around a mouthful of tortilla chips.

"Not me," Annette said, crunching on some popcorn.

"I had them somewhere." Sunshine shifted the six-pack of Coke that was on her lap, and several chocolate bars fell to the floor.

"I might have them," Jessica said. She moved

the small mountain of fashion magazines by her elbow and rifled around in her shopping bag. "Here you go." She tossed a pound bag of the candy toward Bev.

"Pass me some red ones," Annette said as she struggled to get comfortable on the lounge chair. "I don't eat green or brown."

"They all taste the same!" Bev exclaimed as she rooted through the bag. "Here you go." She held out a fistful of red M&M's toward a grateful Annette.

"Oof!" Jessica grunted as Annette's boots collided with her stomach. "Maybe we should try and sneak into the VIP lounge."

"Oh no." Bev shook her head decisively. "I've had *enough* sneaking around, thank you. Look where it gets you!" She swept her arms wide, indicating the seedy airport lounge. "From now on I run a straight race. I don't like having to sleep on an airport bench."

"It's not my idea of paradise either," Sunshine grumbled. She tried lying down across two chairs and yelped when the armrests jabbed her in the back. "I'm starting to miss my bed in the barracks, lumpy mattress and all!"

"Yeah, well, FSSA was sure in a hurry to get rid of us. You'd think we all carried deadly viruses or something!" Annette said bitterly before she opened one of the cans of soda and took a long swallow. "I mean, they could have let us spend the night in the barracks instead of dumping us in the airport."

Jessica nodded in agreement as she reached for some chocolate. At first she'd been only too happy to be free of FSSA. She was so ashamed of her dismissal, she couldn't imagine spending another minute at the compound. And she'd been so busy throwing everything together that she hadn't really had time to think about what was happening to her.

Besides, the airport was fun at first. Jessica sighed. The girls had had a blast hitting all the shops and stocking up on all the junk food that they'd been denied at FSSA. *At first it was kind of like we were having a slumber party,* Jessica thought. But as the clock ticked toward 3 A.M. the charm of unlimited candy and potato chips was beginning to wear thin and the reality of the situation was starting to sink in. *Now it's more like we're pulling an all-nighter before a calculus exam,* Jessica realized with a frown as she surveyed the tense faces of her girlfriends.

"Well, even though they rushed us out of there, they sure found the time to get their tuition back," Bev grumbled, tossing the M&M's aside.

"They made you turn over the money too?" Annette quirked an eyebrow. "The only thing they let me keep was this stupid jumpsuit!"

"You're kidding!" Jessica exclaimed. "I thought *I* was the only one! After I finished packing, they hustled me to the office and demanded I sign over the rest of my scholarship money."

"You were on scholarship too?" Bev, Sunshine, and Annette said in unison. The four girls looked at each other in amazement.

"Something's fishy," Bev continued. "Why would they give us *all* scholarships and then take it *all* back? It doesn't make sense."

"What I want to know is how Phipps found out about the loaded gloves." Sunshine bit down on a cigar and looked fierce.

"Hey, don't look at me like that!" Bev protested. "Do you think I *wanted* to be kicked out?"

"Someone sold us out, that's for sure." Annette looked back and forth between her girl-friends.

"It couldn't have been any one of us," Jessica said, her brow wrinkling in thought. "I mean, from the time the fight ended to the time we were hauled on the carpet in front of Phipps, we were never out of each other's sight. It *had* to be someone else." She waved a potato chip for emphasis.

Am I so sure of that? she wondered, the potato chip dangling hesitantly. *We* were *in each other's company the whole time, but what do I know? I know that these girls all have records,* that's *what. Can I really trust them?* Jessica looked at the faces of the friends she had come to know and love over the past week, doubt clouding her sea green eyes.

"But *who?*" Sunshine persisted. She rifled through her bag, pulled out a sweater, and wrapped it around her like a blanket.

"Oh, who cares," Bev said disconsolately. "The important thing is that our careers in the security business are over before they even had a chance to get started."

She's right, and it's all my fault! Jessica thought, feeling terribly guilty. *After all, the only reason we're all sleeping in a filthy airport is because of me!*

"Look on the bright side," Annette said perkily. She sat up in her chair and propped her boots on the low table in front of her, causing a rainbow of M&M's to scatter on the floor.

"What bright side?" Bev muttered.

"No Pruitt?" Annette suggested.

"*Hot* showers, *fluffy* towels, and *edible* food," Sunshine offered.

Bev shrugged. "I guess I can handle the thought of not seeing Pruitt every morning."

I'd almost rather face Pruitt every day and twice on Sundays than see the looks on my parents' faces when I show up today! Jessica shivered as she thought of how disappointed they would be with her. *How can I tell them that I was dishonorably discharged after I begged and pleaded with them to let me go? They're going to kill me!*

Jessica moaned softly as she imagined the speech her father would give her. She knew it

218

would make Commander Phipps's little talk seem like a Girl Scout lecture. She huddled miserably in her chair. *If only Elizabeth were back in Sweet Valley,* she thought, pangs of loneliness and separation surging through her. *She'd be able to calm Mom and Dad down. They always listen to her.* In fact, she wished she could talk to her sister right now. But when she glanced at her watch, she saw it was four in the morning.

I can't call her now; I'll wake up Tish, and she'll *call Mom and Dad faster than you can say aromawhatever!* Jessica lamented. *If only I could just talk to Elizabeth for a minute. She always makes things better. . . .*

Jessica sat bolt upright and nearly laughed aloud at her cluelessness. *What's my problem?* she asked herself. *I'm in an airport and I have an exchangeable ticket. . . . Who says I have to go to Sweet Valley?*

Jessica sprang to her feet with a surge of energy.

"What are you doing?" Sunshine asked wearily.

"Changing my future," Jessica replied firmly. Gripping her ticket in her fist, she marched purposefully to the reservations counter.

"Can I help you?" the clerk on duty asked between yawns.

"Yes, I'd like to exchange this ticket." Jessica thrust the crumpled voucher across the counter. "I'd like the next flight out of here, please . . . to New York. One way to New York."

Chapter Fifteen

"Tickets?"

"Check. No! Wait a minute—I don't see them!" Elizabeth flung the contents of her purse all over Tom's bed. "They're not here, Tom!"

Tom looked up from the checklist he'd prepared the night before. *Poor Elizabeth, I don't think I've ever seen her this rattled,* he noted. "Forgive me for asking . . . but what's that in your hand?"

Elizabeth looked down at the tickets she was tightly clutching and heaved an enormous sigh of relief.

"Money?" Tom asked.

"Check. No! Where's my wallet? My wallet isn't here!" Elizabeth shrieked. She looked at Tom in shock as she rifled through the mess on the bed.

"What's that on the floor?" Tom bent to retrieve Elizabeth's wallet.

221

"Oh, OK." Elizabeth held her hand to her chest as if she were afraid she was having a heart attack. She grabbed the wallet and stuffed it back in her bag.

"Well, I think that's everything, then." Tom double-checked his list to make sure that he wasn't forgetting anything. Dawn was breaking in the clear Sunday morning sky; their plane was in a couple of hours, and the car service he'd hired was due any minute. They'd already shared their good-byes and good lucks with Tish the night before, and now Tom didn't want to leave anything behind out of carelessness.

"Do you have everything you need for your carry-on bag?" he asked as he zipped up a suitcase.

"My sweater. I need a sweater. It gets cold on the plane," Elizabeth babbled. She raced toward the door and collided with a chest of drawers, which sent her sprawling to the floor.

Tom dusted her off gently and raised her to her feet as if she were a little girl. *I just hope that she feels better once we find out what happened to Jessica,* he thought grimly, his heart swelling with compassion. He smoothed her hair away from her beautiful golden face, which was uncharacteristically twisted in a tense expression. He loved her so much; he hated to see her so unhappy—and so scattered.

"Slow down a second," Tom said softly. He drew Elizabeth into the warm circle of his arms.

"Did I tell you yet this morning how much I love you?"

"Only about ten times." Elizabeth's expression softened slightly, but her brow was still anxious.

"And what about how happy I am that we made up?"

"Hmmm . . ." She pretended to count on her fingers. "I think you only mentioned that about six times." She jumped nearly ten feet in the air as a loud buzzing sound filled the room. "What was that?"

"The doorbell." Tom reluctantly released Elizabeth. "The car service must be here. C'mon, we don't want to miss the plane." He put an arm around Elizabeth and shepherded her out of the room.

We're on our way, he thought as they waited in the foyer for the elevator. *Soon this whole mess will be behind us—and as far as I'm concerned, not a moment too soon!*

"The phone!" Elizabeth gasped just as the elevator doors began to close. "I hear the phone ringing, Tom!"

"OK, OK, Tish's machine will pick it up," Tom replied soothingly.

"No!" Elizabeth lunged for the doors. "It might be Jess!" She flung herself out of the elevator. "Where are my keys?" she yelled, fumbling with the door. After a brief struggle in which her bag, sweater, and keys went flying, Elizabeth flung open the door and raced to the phone. "Hello?" she panted.

"Is this Elizabeth?"

Elizabeth was so overwrought that she couldn't immediately place the snooty voice on the other end of the phone. *It's not Jessica, that's all I know*, she thought with a sinking heart.

"Elizabeth, it's Hildy."

Just what I don't *need*, Elizabeth thought with a groan. She saw out of the corner of her eye that Tom was tapping his foot impatiently. "What is it, Hildy?" Elizabeth asked in exasperation.

"I just wanted to let you know that I'm quitting your play."

"Excuse me?" Elizabeth asked, only half comprehending. Her mind was too filled with worries about her sister to care about anything else.

"I said, I'm *quitting*," Hildy repeated stridently. "I don't feel that our styles *mesh*, Elizabeth. I'm going to work with Claire instead. We've talked it over, and we both agree that my talents will be better showcased in her play. After all, it's so much *bigger* and *edgier*." Hildy paused as if she was expecting Elizabeth to express her outrage. "Did you hear what I said, Elizabeth?" she asked incredulously. "I'm quitting your play. I'm going to be taking Vince's role. It will be a stretch for me, but I must say that will be refreshing after *stagnating* in the role of Phoebe."

"That's nice," Elizabeth said vaguely, smiling at the gasp of shock and disappointment on the other end of the line. *Does she expect me to care?* she wondered. *Even if I liked her, it wouldn't matter right now. I have bigger things to worry about.* Elizabeth looked at her watch. "Listen, Hildy, I can't talk now. Nice working with you!" Elizabeth hung up the phone on Hildy's outraged squawking.

"Let's rock and roll," Tom said, holding open the door. "From now on we don't stop for *anything*, OK?"

Fine with me! Elizabeth thought as she stepped into the elevator once more.

Jessica stretched out luxuriously against the soft fabric of her seat and took a sip of Perrier. Some awesomely cute guy had insisted on giving her his seat in first class, and she had gratefully accepted. Now that she had had time to catch up on her beauty magazines, she began to reflect on just what had gone down at FSSA.

Something tells me that Pruitt wasn't totally on the up-and-up, she thought as she flipped through one of her magazines. *Just what were all those printouts in her office anyway? Why was she so interested in the sharpshooters? Is she from some kind of terrorist organization?* Jessica felt goose bumps rise on her arms.

And just who was the "unnamed source" anyway? Pruitt? she asked herself. *Had she set me up all along? Did she know that I was going to pack my punch and go along with it just so I would be expelled?*

Jessica sipped her Perrier with a thoughtful look on her face as she went over the chain of events in her mind. Could it have been Sunshine? Bev? Annette? Could they have hated FSSA so much that they would have wanted to get expelled? Jessica frowned. That didn't make sense at all. The place was pretty grim, but they could have just walked if they wanted to.

And what was all that jazz with the scholarship money anyway? she wondered. It seemed like too much of a coincidence that all four of them would have received it—especially when past arrest records were involved. *Would FSSA go through the trouble of offering scholarship money to* everybody? *And if so—why?*

Jessica's mind went around in circles, but try as she might, she couldn't come up with any answers that made sense. "Well, at least one good thing came out of this mess," she murmured lightly. "I got out of there in one piece!"

The speakers above her crackled. "We are now making our descent into La Guardia Airport," the captain began, interrupting Jessica's train of thought.

Jessica turned and looked excitedly out the window at the island of Manhattan. Even from far up in the air, it still looked huge. *Just think,*

226

there're a million fabulous boutiques down there, she thought excitedly. *A trillion great beauty salons, a gazillion cute guys—and best of all, Elizabeth!*

She felt better already.

"Which gate do you think it is?" Elizabeth asked Tom anxiously as she scanned the monitors listing arrivals and departures.

"I don't know," Tom admitted with a frown. "You stay here. I'm going to the information desk to see what I can find out." He left his carry-on bag with Elizabeth and sprinted purposefully away.

I hope the plane isn't delayed or anything, Elizabeth thought worriedly. *That's the last thing I need.* She moved slightly to the right to check out another bunch of monitors on the far wall. "Whoops! Excuse me," Elizabeth mumbled as she absentmindedly bumped into someone's suitcase. "I was just . . . Vince! What are you doing here?" she asked in disbelief.

"Taking a plane, the same as you." Vince's dark eyes twinkled. "Seriously, I'm cutting and running. I've left the play, Elizabeth."

"Did you know that Hildy's taken your part?" Elizabeth said with an impish grin.

Vince shrugged, bemused. "I couldn't care less." His expression turned thoughtful as he stared at Elizabeth. "There is one thing I do care about, though."

Elizabeth flushed under the intensity of his gaze. She could guess what was coming next.

"I realized after we kissed . . . you were the only reason I was staying with the Miller Huttleby program. I can handle getting slammed by *The Hollywood Page,* and I can deal with getting cussed out by my agent." He reached for Elizabeth's hand. "I'd thought I was afraid to quit because of those things. But they had nothing to do with it. I was holding out for you."

"I'm sorry, Vince," Elizabeth said softly.

"Hey, it's OK." Vince smiled. "But how about a hug for the road?"

"Of course." Elizabeth returned his smile and stepped into his arms. *This is the way a hug should feel—from a friend,* she mused. *It's nothing compared to the way it feels when Tom holds me.*

I must be dreaming—scratch that; I must be having a nightmare! Tom fumed as he looked on, stunned, from his position at the information counter. Vince Klee had just swept Elizabeth into a dramatic embrace that wouldn't have looked out of place in an old-time Hollywood movie. *Who does he think he is? Clark Gable? Did he call Tish and find out where we were? Is he hoping to persuade her to leave me and fly to the Bahamas with him?*

Tom stalked angrily from the information counter back to where Elizabeth and Vince stood. *I'm not going to let this guy get to me,* he vowed, but not without noting bitterly how Vince's formfitting T-shirt left little to the imagination. *I'm going to act mature—after I surgically remove his arms from around my girlfriend, that is. What's he going to do about it? He's at least five inches shorter than I am!*

"Tom," Elizabeth said brightly as he approached. She disengaged herself from Vince's arms and nestled herself against Tom. Tom gathered her close; resting his chin on her head, he glowered at Vince.

"Isn't this an amazing coincidence? I never would have expected to run into Vince here!" Elizabeth exclaimed.

"Yeah, what a coincidence," he said shortly.

"Vince is on his way back to California," Elizabeth continued.

"Really?" Tom perked up considerably. "You're leaving the city? What about the play?"

"I'm quitting," Vince replied.

"What a shame." Tom tried to interject some sincerity into his words, but he couldn't stop himself from grinning broadly.

Things are definitely looking up! he thought, his heart soaring. *Vince is leaving, we're going to find Jessica, and Elizabeth is back where she belongs—in* my *arms!*

"Well, good luck in California, Vince," Elizabeth said, snug in the comforting circle of Tom's arms.

229

"You too." Vince nodded and reached down to pick up his bag. "After all, if you decide to stay with the play, you need all the luck you can get."

"That's true," Elizabeth retorted wryly. "At least I won't have to deal with Hildy anymore, now that she's decided to replace you." Elizabeth laughed. "I guess you're really doing me a favor by leaving."

"I'm always happy to oblige you, Elizabeth," Vince said smoothly. "Let me know what happens with *Two Sides to Every Story*." He paused for a second. "Good-bye, Eliz—"

"Elizabeth!"

Elizabeth whirled around, her heart pounding wildly. *Could it be*—

"Who said that?" Vince asked, looking around.

"It came from over there." Tom pointed to the arrival lounge.

"I'm seeing things!" Vince gasped.

Elizabeth, elated beyond belief, sped as quickly as her feet could take her to the concourse entrance to meet the joyful sight with the rumpled black jumpsuit and tousled hair. "Jessica!" Elizabeth shrieked. "Oh, thank goodness, you're all right!"

"Liz!" Jessica flung herself into her sister's arms. They held on to each other as if they would never let go.

"I was so worried about you!" Elizabeth wept

230

into her sister's hair. "I was on my way to Miami to get you, I was so scared."

"I barely got out of FSSA alive," Jessica wailed. "You don't know what it was like! The food was awful, there weren't any cute guys, I ran out of makeup, I almost got killed by my psycho drill sergeant. . . . Oh, it was horrible. Just horrible." Jessica shuddered as she allowed Elizabeth to lead her back to where Tom was waiting.

Elizabeth laughed in relief. "It sounds pretty bad—but I should have known you would come out on top." Elizabeth shook her head and squeezed her sister's arm. "Look at you—you've got no stitches or anything. I had imagined—"

"Stitches?" Jessica stared at her sister as if she were crazy. "You know, I haven't had a manicure for ages, I've probably got *permanent sun damage*—long-term effects, Liz. Think of the long-term effects."

Elizabeth slowed down and smiled as they reached the monitors. "Jess, there's someone I'd like you to meet."

Jessica's jaw dropped open. She stood stock-still and stared. For once she was speechless.

Now I really know there was something fishy going on at FSSA, Jessica realized. *Obviously they poisoned the water or something. Why else would I be hallucinating? Although as hallucinations go, this one is pretty good!*

Jessica couldn't believe her eyes. Vince Klee's biceps were even more awesome than she'd ever envisioned, and she'd envisioned them—*a lot. Of course they're awesome,* she reasoned. *I'm imagining them, and I have a* great *imagination!*

Fully gratified, Jessica realized that Vince Klee was staring at her as if she were the most beautiful blonde in creation. *Well, what do you know,* she noted. *My hallucination even has good taste!*

"Jessica?" Elizabeth prompted. "Aren't you going to say hello to Vince? I thought you were such a fan." She nudged Jessica with her elbow.

Jessica turned to her sister, flabbergasted. *You mean I'm not imagining him? He's* real? She whirled back around and gaped. *He must be!* she realized, her heart thumping wildly. *Elizabeth's much too straitlaced to be having the same sexy hallucination. Besides, I always pictured him to be a little taller. . . .*

"You're really Vince Klee?" she stammered at last. "I've been fantasizing about saving your life for weeks!" Jessica dropped her knapsack and stared at him, dumbstruck.

"Well . . ." Vince flashed a killer smile, took her hand, and looked deeply into her eyes. "In that case, maybe I should forget about my plane because I could *definitely* use some lifesaving right now."

How would you feel about a little mouth-to-mouth resuscitation? Jessica wondered, her eyes twinkling mischievously.

Can Elizabeth convince Jessica and Vince to join her play? Or will they be too busy partying to care? Find out in Sweet Valley University #41, **ESCAPE TO NEW YORK.**